WITHDRAWN

CONTEMPORARY

LATIN AMERICAN CLASSICS

◆

J. Cary Davis, *General Editor*

The Poisoned Water
El agua envenenada

FERNANDO BENÍTEZ

Translated by Mary E. Ellsworth

Foreword by J. Cary Davis

SOUTHERN ILLINOIS UNIVERSITY PRESS
Carbondale and Edwardsville

Feffer & Simons, Inc.
London and Amsterdam

Library of Congress Cataloging in Publication Data

Benítez, Fernando, 1911–
    The poisoned water.

    (Contemporary Latin American classics)
    I. Title.
PZ3.B432Po3 [PQ7297.B325]   863   74–184549
ISBN 0–8093–0634–4

FOREWORD

The Author

Fernando Benítez (1912–) is a Professor of Journalism in the Facultad de Ciencias Políticas y Sociales of the Universidad Nacional Autónoma of Mexico. He has won numerous awards, including the Premio Mazatlán for the best book published in 1968. He has traveled widely, having covered the opening sessions of the United Nations in San Francisco as a reporter, following which he visited Latin America, Europe in general and the Soviet Union in particular, the Mideast and China, writing feature stories on his impressions and interviews with various personalities in these areas.

Professor Benítez's journalistic endeavors are impressive: collaborator on the *Revista de Revistas* (1934–36); reporter, editorial writer, and editor of the well-known Mexican daily, *El Nacional* (1936–47); editor and founder of the English language *Daily News* (1947), as well as several other supplements to newspapers in the capital and the periodical *Siempre*. He has had hundreds of articles published in dozens of magazines and newspapers in Mexico. In 1947 he was adviser to UNESCO in the field of journalism, and was decorated that same year by the French government for his journalistic work during the war.

Benítez's first publications include selections and the foreword to a Spanish edition of Eckermann's *Conversations with Goethe* (Espasa Calpe, 1943); a collection of short stories titled *Caballo y Dios* (1945); *La ruta de Hernán Cortés* (1950), subsequently translated into English (1952, 1957) and German (1955); a play, *Cristóbal Colón* (1953) which was presented at the Palacio de Bellas Artes on occasion of the quadricentennial of the National University of Mexico;

a history, *La vida criolla en el siglo XVI* (1953), republished under the title of *Los primeros Mexicanos* (1962) and translated into English (1965), French (1970). His other publications are many: *China a la vista* (1953), *Ki, el drama de un pueblo y una planta* (1956), *La batalla de Cuba* (1960; Polish translation same year), *Viaje a la Tarahumara* (1960) (Russian translation 1963), *La ruta de la libertad* (1960, to commemorate the 150th anniversary of Independence), *La última trinchera* (1963), *Los hongos alucinantes* (1964) (Italian edition 1972), *Los Indios de México* (3 vols. 1967, 1968, 1970 with translations into Italian, Polish, English, and French). Benítez's first novel, *El rey viejo* (1959), has appeared in editions in Serbo-Croatian (1964), Polish (1965), Ukrainian (1965), French (1965). All these works have had several printings.

The Book

The first edition of *El agua envenenada* appeared in 1961, with a special edition in England for students of Spanish (1967). As the reader of this English edition will discover, it deals with the exploitation of an Indian village in Michoacán by the local boss, and the consequent uprising of the people when the rumor spreads that he has poisoned the villagers' only source of water. Events lead inevitably to a violent, bloody conclusion, with the future of the village in doubt. The basic plot logically invites comparison to that of Icaza's *Huasipungo* (published in English as *The Villagers,* Southern Illinois University Press, 1964), but the treatment is quite different. The story of *The Poisoned Water* is narrated, as a report to his bishop, by the local priest, who was eyewitness to the events and had tried to act as an intermediary in the quarrel between the villagers and the boss, being present when the latter's household was attacked, but unable to prevent his murder by the irate populace. The stark realism of *Huasipungo* is absent. Nevertheless, the story is well told and gradually builds to a powerful climax which cannot fail to hold the reader's attention.

The novel is based on actual happenings, and the author lived for a while in the village where the events took place, interviewing the principal actors in the drama. He says that he wrote the book to show "el poder de los caciques en América para todo tipo de lector."

The Translator

Mary E. Ellsworth now lives in Naples, Florida. She has a B.S. degree in Library Science from the University of Minnesota (1938), with additional majors and minors in History, Latin, and Economics. She lists for herself three distinct careers: (1) as assistant in the Minneapolis Public Library, for five years; (2) more than twenty-two years with the Federal Aviation Administration (dealing with air-ground radio, meteorology, pilot briefing, and other on-the-ground phases of nonairline aviation)—much of this period at Purdue University Airport; and (3) since her retirement, translation work. Her basic language courses in college, together with auditions of Spanish lectures at Purdue (1965–67), plus travel in Spain (1966) have given her ample background for doing the translation of *The Poisoned Water*. She has additional translations from Spanish and Portuguese, more of which deserve to see the light of day if we are to judge by the quality of the present work.

J. CARY DAVIS
Professor Emeritus Romance Languages

San Juan Capistrano
June 1972

The Poisoned Water

I

I received Your Grace's order on Friday, and on Sunday, at eight o'clock in the morning, I was crossing the atrium of the cathedral. I confess that it is not easy for a village priest to be called into the presence of his archbishop, especially after the terrible events in which I unavoidably took part in a manner I find difficult to explain.

I spent a very anxious night. I was continually consulting my watch, and the imminence of the interview—it was to take place in the chapter room after mass—prevented me from putting my ideas in order or finding arguments to justify my conduct in your eyes.

It had rained all night. The laurel trees, freed of the winter's accumulation of dust, provided that contrast, familiar since my long-ago seminary days, between their fresh, dark, close-set branches and the dry pinkish stone of the cathedral. As the last note of the bell sounded, the ringing for Easter Week began. I seemed to smell the strips of badly tanned sheepskin that held the broken clapper together, and I listened with a twenty-year-old heart to the solemn lament of the largest bell, which is inscribed with Latin words in raised letters, swelling and bursting like a golden bubble in the thin morning air.

Soon the hand bells turned on their shafts, the smaller bells joined in the concert, and these sounds flew like birds into the shining nave and surrounded the faithful who were standing on the pavement, lifting their faces alive with joy toward the towers. Once more they firmly believed that Christ's victory was their victory and that His resurrection had rescued them from death, transforming them into gods.

When I entered the cathedral, the mass *In Albis* was beginning, and the celebrant was pronouncing the words of the Introit, bending over his missal: *"Quasi modo geniti infantes, alleluia."*

I looked for a place near the presbytery and settled down to hear the mass. I could not concentrate. For the first time in twenty-five years I was outside that privileged enclosure which forms the presbytery, the transept, and the choir—a cathedral within the cathedral—and I was attending the holy sacrifice standing among the worshippers. From my place I observed the sexton's frayed trousers showing below his tunic and the music master directing the ceremony, silver baton in hand.

That was my proper atmosphere. An atmosphere smelling of incense and fading flowers, where the marquetry floors of the choir, the ancient polished wood and the vestment brocades softly reflect the brilliance of chandeliers and of wax candles set in tall candelabras. I could open the choir book precisely at the psalm the choir was singing and indicate the exact spot in the presbytery where I had lain full-length, face down, like a dead man, on the day of my ordination.

Sitting on your archbishop's throne and half hidden by clouds of incense, Your Grace was also part of the cathedral and part of those innocent days that I was remembering only to compare them with my present deterioration and the agitated state in which I found myself.

The years, Monsignor, have scarcely touched you. Your wide dark face with prominent cheekbones, bathed in perspiration, remained motionless, crowned by your miter; your two hands in white gloves embroidered with crosses rested on your knees, and your Indian eyes, hard and impenetrable, brought you to mind, more than any other symbol of authority, as the severe judge of my youth. I thought again of the dreaded interview. Now I was sure that I would not be able to tell rationally the story in which I was involved. It was too obscure and improbable to be told in the brief time allotted me, and the children's choir, as they intoned the psalm *Dixit Dominus,* ended by confusing me: *"Judicabit in nationibus, implebit ruinas, conquassabit capita in terra multorum."*

God had fulfilled His threat: "He judged the nations, He brought about their ruin, and He shattered the heads of many on the ground," but why did He select my little flock for delivering His blow and not other cities where the abominations are greater?

I do not pretend, Monsignor, to fathom the designs of the Almighty. I tried to say with the apostle, "My Lord and My God," but the images which the reading of the Epistle aroused in me—the doubting of Thomas called Didymus—and the scenes of horror I had witnessed were mixed in my weakened brain: "Reach forth thy hand and thrust it into my side, and be not faithless but believing." The wound burned with a strange fire, and as I felt it burning, I hastened, full of compassion, to withdraw it.

The blood that flowed from his side stained my cassock and formed a reddish mist through which I saw men topple over and their innocent or guilty heads shatter on the ground.

2

The confusion of a great solemn occasion prevailed in the brightly lighted vestry. The rustling Chinese damasks of the chasubles and the raincoats were tossed into chests of drawers. The fleshy, rounded figures who escort the Emperor Constantine's chariot in the large central painting evoked a sensual pomp. They created, if I may say so, the reflection of a pagan, mythological world without any relation to, or any possible link with, the priests busy changing clothes, or with the acolytes and sacristans carrying missals and wine cruets who were darting from side to side.

The bustle upset my nerves, which were in need of silence. Why should I lie to you? I wanted to escape, to postpone the imminent judgment, and I was already sidling toward the door when the unmistakable murmur that announces the arrival of a high dignitary obliged me to stop, and Your Grace appeared on the threshold. You were still wearing your miter; your gloved hand was holding your crosier sparkling with precious stones, and the embroidered vestment that covered you made me think of the image of one of those princes of the church appearing on baroque altars, who by some miraculous circumstance might have descended from his pedestal.

As is their custom, the aristocracy of the city surrounded you. Old merchants who had become rich by a monopoly of wheat and corn for generations, retired shopkeepers, feudal gentlemen whom the revolution had dispossessed of their farms were undertaking, with the church's support, to revive the splendor of other days. They, too, were the reflection of a bygone era. Their robes embroidered with the red cross of Saint James were rumpled; their faded Holy Sepulcher uniforms smelled of mothballs; and the feathers on their hats were moth-eaten and shabby. Time, that had dealt so relentlessly with these items in their wardrobes, had on the other hand preserved their rapacious little eyes, their drooping soft noses, and though luxury had remained far from their cold, sunken lips, they still retained the unmistakable stamp of the guest who occupied them for so many years.

Your Grace's glance was fastened upon me for a moment. Undoubtedly you had forgotten me, and besides, no one could have identified the priest of Tajimaroa, whose name apparently figured on the front pages of the newspapers, with the little black-clad man who was trying to pass unnoticed.

3

Five minutes after I left the vestry, one of the servants touched my arm, saying:

"Monsignor is waiting for you in the chapter room."

At the rear of this venerable, familiar room where the portraits of dead archbishops are hung, Your Grace was seated at the table on which breakfast had been laid.

"Well," you said in your harsh voice, in which vibrated your old note of ironic heartiness, "what does this conspiring priest have to tell me?"

I felt your reception—I must be perfectly frank with you—like a blow.

"Your Grace," I replied, upset, "I am no conspirator," and I thoughtlessly added, "my enemies . . ."

You quickly interrupted me:

"You don't know yourself how many enemies you have!"

My eyes focused on the table, and since I was unable to prevent it, saliva flowed into my mouth. On the repoussé silver tray lay a glass of orange juice, a cup of chocolate, and a little basket filled with rolls which peeped out from between the artistically folded corners of the napkin.

Your Grace did not want to let this weakness in my character pass unnoticed—I have never been able to conquer it in spite of my efforts—and you asked, accentuating your mocking joviality:

"Perhaps you have not breakfasted?"

"Oh, yes, Monsignor," I hastened to answer, swallowing my saliva.

Your Grace finished drinking your juice and, giving proof of your privileged memory, took up the thread of the inquisition again:

"I am going to tell you how many enemies you have, since you mentioned them. In the first place, you have the rela-

tives of the victims, or putting it more clearly, of the murdered men."

"I don't understand you, Monsignor. I did the unspeak-
able thing in order to save their lives."

"They speak of your inciting the people against each
other."

"That is a slander."

"In any case, you could not or would not protect them
adequately, as was your duty."

"I was alone facing ten thousand enraged men!"

You hesitated a moment, the cup of chocolate in your hand,
and said before raising it to your lips:

"I want to remind you, father, that those ten thousand
enraged men are your parishioners. A part of the flock I entrusted to you."

I could not think of a suitable reply and kept silent. Your
Grace turned around in your chair and looked out of the
corner of your eyes, intensely and fearfully, at the niche in
the bare wall next to the last archbishop. Perhaps you looked
at that niche casually, but I imagined that you had been
attracted by that small indentation where, according to the
rules, they will hang your picture after you die. The empty
niche in question was the only one in that large room, and
among the portraits of the forty prelates preceding you that
extended all along the walls, it stood out conspicuously, like
the empty space a tooth leaves in a beautiful mouth, and this
hollow space attracted your attention more than did the
remaining portraits in which the old archbishops, sumptu-
ously dressed, their hand supported on the table holding their
miter, formed a chain of shadow in which one link was missing, and that link was yourself, the only living man—I saw
you move your muscles under the skin of your shaven cheeks
—the one who seemed to point up the others' lack of life, as
if Your Grace were indeed a man summoned, a man condemned to death, by that niche in the wall which so im-
periously, so eagerly demanded your presence.

4

Forgive me. Forgive my incoherence, my foolishness, my repeated digressions. In writing this statement which Your Grace is to take as the general confession of the least of his priests, I have promised myself to hide nothing from you and to reveal my thoughts to you no matter how absurd they may appear.

I must have turned pale—I actually did feel faint—because the tone of your voice became sweeter, and you spoke affectionately to me:

"Sit down. You are tired."

I recovered somewhat and tried to concentrate.

"I understand your scruples, Monsignor. It is not often a priest finds himself involved in a tale of blood and violence."

"You did not do much to stop the evil. Moreover, I have reasons for believing you secretly encouraged it."

"The day of wrath had come, and I was swept away with the others, because of my sins, certainly."

"Let us understand each other, señor cura," Your Grace replied, letting a slight irritation show through. "I do not like my priests to set themselves up as prophets. Times have changed . . . Your prophecies went beyond the limits of the Old Testament and fell under police jurisdiction."

"The Lord is always the same," I ventured to say almost inaudibly.

"You are using a language in which we will not be able to understand each other. I do not hold you responsible for the events that took place in Tajimaroa. I accuse you—yes, I do accuse you—of a certain complacency, of an inadmissible fatalism, and that is also the judgment of the authorities. I am trying to help you, to save you in the final instance from jail, and you come here telling me that the day of wrath had arrived and that you got carried away because of your sins!"

"Don't condemn me, Your Grace, before you've listened to me. Today I'm not in any condition to defend myself."

"There is not much more I want to add. There are difficult parishes—with men rebelling and leaving the church—but that is not the case in your parish. Tell me, aren't your parishioners docile?"

"Yes, they are docile, Monsignor."

"Do they not obey you? Do they not respect your office?"

"They're obedient and only too respectful."

"One more question. Do you not have power over them?"

"My power is limited, like all powers."

"Very well. Pay attention to what I'm going to tell you. Yesterday I carefully reread the reports which your predecessors in the parish left us. They cover more than twenty years, and both agree with you. But there is a difference. In those twenty years only one deplorable event took place, one single case of rebellion which they were not able to put down in time. Both of them knew how to keep control over the parishioners, and when one of them died—you ought to know this—the whole town felt that its father and shepherd had died, and they all came weeping to his funeral. The other priest, promoted to the dignity of an abbot three years ago, is still remembered in Tajimaroa, and people undertake long journeys only if they receive his advice and blessing. In regard to you . . ."

A servant approached to whisper:

"It's time for the confirmations, Monsignor. The people have been waiting for half an hour."

"It has got late," Your Grace declared, pushing back the lace sleeve of your vestment and looking at your watch, "but I will be finished in five minutes. Only five minutes more. In regard to you," you continued imperturbably, "I must point out that you have not done honor to the example of your predecessors. The people complain about you, as the victims' families complain, and the authorities, though they have other reasons. These reasons, if they do indeed benefit you to a certain extent, do not alter the lamentable fact that there is a unanimous feeling against you, that they have all been turned into your enemies. Tell me, tell me at once," you exclaimed, tapping the floor with your embroidered sandal, "what evidence I must present in order to clear you."

"The story is long and complicated, Monsignor, and it would take a great deal of time . . ."

"Not more than five minutes."

"That is impossible, but one thing I do want to beg of you again: do not judge me without listening to me."

"What do you propose? A lengthy conversation?"

"Allow me to submit a detailed report of the events to you. A written report."

Your face softened and, patting my shoulder, as you used to do in the seminary after your customary reprimand, you concluded:

"Very well. Go back to Tajimaroa and write it immediately. I want the truth, only the truth, and don't forget that your absolution or condemnation depends on that report."

I fell on my knees and kissed your pastoral ring. As I got up and brushed the dust from my trousers, Your Grace had already disappeared among the crosses, the robes of Saint James and of the Holy Sepulcher, the uniforms, and the shabby feathers that waved on the elderly gentlemen's tricorn hats.

5

Perhaps, Monsignor, it might be fitting to speak of myself for a moment. No, I shall not be too prolix, I assure you. My life lacks unusual events, and if I refer to it, I do so not with the purpose of gaining your benevolence, but with the desire that my story may have a certain unity and may not seem like a mere ghost story.

I was born in 1908 in Zinapécuaro, a town in the mountains. My father, a postal employee and a small-time seller of wood, died before I was eight years old, but his image is linked with my life by a strange event which I wish to relate to you.

One morning I was taking his lunch to the station where he had set up his office when, halfway there, five or six armed men snatched away my basket before I could prevent it. The idea that my father, already very ill at that time, should spend his whole day without food filled me with rage, and I went after them, biting and kicking. Of the fight I remember only that it was soon finished. A blow full in the face dropped me to the ground. Bleeding, I managed to get up, and while they were going off I shouted at them the bad words I was learning at that time from the charcoal sellers, of which I had an inexhaustible supply.

Amused, the men laughed. Soon, as my insults rose in tone, they angrily unslung the rifles which they carried on their shoulders and cocked them. I did not give them a chance to shoot me. In one leap I cleared the hedge bordering the road and, hurling my best insults at them by way of farewell, returned to the town.

On the outskirts I met two of my father's friends. Since they were going to the station to pick up their letters, I decided to accompany them, and I made the trip once more, telling them of my adventure, which they received with peals of laughter, pounding me hard on the back.

I slept that night in the post office. My father had seated himself on the floor, leaning his back against the wall, and I stretched out, resting my head on his legs. Outside we heard cries and shots. He did nothing but stroke my hair and say his rosary in a low voice, but that murmuring set up a defense, a protection, that kept us safe from that nocturnal fight. I think that my religious vocation was fixed upon that night. In later years, every time I lost heart, I would hear my father's murmuring, his prayer falling upon me and annointing me with its grace.

On the following morning we returned to Zinapécuaro. The soldiers who had fought furiously in the darkness had vanished, and from every telegraph pole dangled a corpse. Hurrying his pace, my father told me with a tremor in his voice:

"Don't look. You had better pray for them."

He need not have feared. The spectacle of hanged men— one of the most cruel and shameless appearances with which death is clothed—formed part of my existence and was inserted into it naturally, like the hunger, wrongs, and murders which were, which had to be, the inseparable companions of my life.

When my father died at last—he was at death's door for about a year—my mother was obliged to move us to my grandfather's house. The old man had lost his feet because of gangrene, and he got about very slowly with the aid of two leather pads fastened to his knees and two little crutches above which his mutilated body used to sway.

My grandfather was very religious also. I would frequently come upon him supported on his crutches, absorbed in prayer. He prayed with his eyes closed, and his bodiless face, that face hidden in a long curly beard, was so powerful in its self-communion that it would sadden me to bring him back to reality in order to tell him:

"Grandfather, the charcoal sellers have come from the woods and are waiting in the street."

My grandfather supported himself by buying and selling charcoal, but in those years business had fallen off a great deal. The roads were dangerous because of the revolution, and the people of Zinapécuaro cut their own firewood in the woods, with the result that we were almost always hungry, and we associated that irritating sensation of a hollow which could not be filled, not with the revolution—at that time we did not know the meaning of that word—but with the bandits who called themselves revolutionaries.

From my seventh to eleventh year my principal activity

consisted of carrying out tasks that civilized men have forgotten. I went out very early to the woods in search of mushrooms and herbs, I hunted rabbits and birds and provided our water by bringing it from the public fountain in two empty oil cans. If I were lucky, I would exchange charcoal—those round solid oak trunks that burned with a soft aromatic fire—for garbanzo cakes, lard or a piece of pork, and we would give ourselves the illusion that the good days of peace and plenty had returned to our house. Grandfather—his head scarcely reached above the table—would bless the meal, and my mother would turn aside her thin face and touch her handkerchief to her eyes.

That must have been 1918, the so-called hunger year. In Zinapécuaro, naturally, we did not know anything about the world war. News came from time to time for our important neighbors, but these made no comments, nor were we interested in what was happening on the other side of the ocean because we had a war of our own, and it affected us too much for us to worry about foreign battles.

The revolutionaries did nothing to improve the idea we had formed of them. They robbed or killed among themselves, and when they were not doing those two things, they violated the women, or we would see them sprawled in the sun picking off their fleas.

They came and went in waves. Villa's men, Zapata's, Orozco's, Carranza's, Obregon's occupied the town when they were victorious or abandoned it when they were defeated, and the situation in Zinapécuaro did not improve. They were as ignorant as I myself was of the cause for which they were fighting, and at bottom I despised them, for at that time I was a mere child and did not know that those men—blind, innocent tools of the generals—were unhappier than we.

The revolution formed my character to some extent. Violence taught us to despise danger and to become only too familiar with our condition of being persecuted. I remember very well one morning when I had gone to the plaza for water. My mother, ill with typhoid, was raving:

"Father, see that the boy works. Idleness is bad . . . idleness is very bad . . ." she said to my grandfather, her lips cracked by fever, tossing her head on the pillow.

I filled the cans at the fountain, and as I crossed the plaza again, bent under the weight of the water, a skirmish began. The enemies were out of sight. Hidden in the woods, they began the attack cautiously, and we heard only the dry noise of their shots. The men defending the town turned their backs on me. They peered from behind tree trunks or from the rooftops and fired regularly. Some were smoking, and none seemed excited. I went on my way unafraid. Bullets bounced on the pavement so close to me that two or three perforated my cans, and the water escaped in rivulets, wetting my legs and shoes. Not even this act could frighten me. Without hurrying, I arrived home and threw down the two empty cans in the entryway.

My grandfather saw the holes and took his rosary out of his pocket.

"Now look, grandfather," I exclaimed, furious, "don't send me to the plaza for water. They've ruined the only two cans we've got!"

6

Such was my childhood—not at all bitter or sad, but on the contrary, happy and unworried. We were a gang of tiny marauders, of child vultures who, when a battle was scarcely finished, would go to the battlefield and steal what we could: a silk handkerchief, a general's binoculars, or a soldier's boots.

There was no need to bury the dead. They lay smiling on the field, and the buzzards took care of cleaning them. They began their work with the eyes—birds of prey do not like to eat under the fixed, glassy stare of the dead—went on to the soft flesh of the belly, and finished with disagreeable peckings, eating a little of everything at random, like surfeited gluttons who do not stop swallowing until the last morsels of the banquet have disappeared.

Our principal diversion was that of looking for empty cartridges in the abandoned trenches. With the cartridges and a little stolen powder we fashioned cannons and infernal machines that exploded in the most respectable places, arousing terror in the neighborhood women, cats, and dogs.

We had our little heads full of bellicose dreams, and we could conceive of nothing better than to organize imitation massacres, military trials, and executions, games in which we came to be great experts and played in turn the roles of judge, jailer, and executioner.

Even the cemetery was included in that gamut of varied experience. The marble worker of our town having been drafted—his exchange of chisel for sword was advantageous for him, since he rose to be a general—the son of the cemetery administrator, feeling sorry for our poverty, gave us little jobs. It was an easy, even a pleasant occupation. I would place the marble slab over the grave, sketch the epitaph, and then, with a toothed chisel, bite into the surface of the slab, being very careful not to cut into the blank space reserved for the lettering. While the chisel rang out, the birds sang in the cypress trees, the angels seemed to watch over me sympathetically, and doubt would assail me as to whether I should take up the profession of arms or the gentler one of cutting tombstone marble, since the peace, the dignified orderliness, and the grave silence of that graceful, elegant world certainly could not be compared with the violence, corruption, and the horror of inglorious death which the soldier attained as his only recompense on the field of battle.

I am wasting your time telling you meaningless tales, and Your Grace must forgive me. At the age of fifty-two, our childhood emotions come out of their hiding places and besiege us, reclaiming a place in our life as if, obedient to a natural law, they intend to compensate us for the gray worries of age, its sad images, and its disillusions by the color and innocence of those early days.

Those are the days of Gulliver in the land of the giants, days burdened with secrets to be revealed, when we discover the world, and the little monkey finds an indescribable pleasure in imitating the big monkeys. Innocence unconsciously copies their foolishness and crimes and transforms them into a game. Unfortunately it prolongs their imitation of adult models, and when innocence leaves us, these cease to be games and take on the tragic character of real foolishness and crimes.

With the deaths of my mother and grandfather, occurring close together in 1920, my childhood ended. A paternal uncle, a rectory canon of the cathedral in Morelia, took me by the hand to the seminary, and my passion for arms terminated as rapidly as it had begun.

7

My fifteen years in the seminary—all my youth and the beginning of my maturity—coincided with the most difficult years of the religious persecution. One October day, while I was in class, the bell—or rather, that lament from cracked, badly cast metal—brusquely summoned us to the seminary cloister. There the teachers were gathered in a corner at one end, and the rector's pale face rose, somewhat ghostly, among naked bayonets, like the face of a man condemned to death.

We did not understand what was going on. The rector took a few steps forward, leaving the bayonets behind, and crossing his arms over his chest, said to us in a calm voice:

"The general"—only then did I notice a man in uniform who stood beside him, cleaning his teeth with a toothpick—"advises me that we must leave our house. It is an injustice"—hearing the word, the general took the toothpick out of his mouth and said something which no one understood, but the rector, extending his arm authoritatively, repeated, "it is an injustice against which we cannot rebel. Go to your dormitories, pack your suitcases, and return to the courtyard so that we may all leave together." Then, turning to the general, he added, "Your display of force, general, is unnecessary and ridiculous. You could have come alone and spared your soldiers that embarrassment. For us it is not the first injustice, nor will it be the last."

Our rector spoke prophetically. From that moment on we were scattered, without tonsure or cassock, house or breviary. Becoming frightened, many seminarians deserted; others sought refuge in seminaries abroad, and although I was offered the opportunity of studying in San Antonio, Texas, I steadfastly refused, feeling that one same destiny should unite the boy who kept on walking across the plaza at Zinapécuaro with his riddled water cans with the youth who leaped the hedges to flee from the soldiers and government bloodhounds.

Ah, Monsignor, how many times from the top of the ridge we looked hopefully at the village which was to be our refuge stretching into the valley! The smoke escaping from the ash gray roofs smelled of oak—those thick, firm trunks that I used to exchange for garbanzo cakes—and the nearness of our new home filled my eyes with tears. The townspeople stood on the worn stone sidewalk, waiting for us, and as I passed in front of the closed church door, I promised myself that I should be the first to open it, with flowers and hosannas, and my consecrated hands should be the ones to replace the Lord on His empty altar.

And the surprises of our relocation! Chapel in the salon, classroom in the dining room, cells in the granaries. During recreation periods we would sing while we planted cabbages and lettuce; we studied energetically, surrounded by mockingbirds and geraniums on the porch. Life began again; the Gospel and Virgil, Saint Augustine and Cicero revealed to

us the meaning of charity and beauty; examinations were announced, but one afternoon the master of the house would
appear, beside himself.

"The federals are coming!" he would cry. "Somebody has
denounced us."

We would have to flee. I would slip away into the country
and hide in a tree, in a haystack, in the dry bed of an arroyo.
It was beautiful to stretch out on the grass, to contemplate
the intense life of the sky, and think of the church's superi-
ority, invulnerable in its destiny.

The wind of hate dragged us with it and made us whirl
madly. Nothing mattered. That period, like that of my childhood, with its pains, its privations, and its bitternesses, holds
such seduction, shines so vividly in my memory, that I am
like a pillar of salt turned toward its powerful flames, a man
subdued and absorbed in front of that fragment of my past
that was the clandestine mass, the communion carried secretly to the sick, the Christmas songs resounding joyfully
in the prisons of remote country towns.

8

A short time before my ordination, I spent my last vacation
in Zinapécuaro. My suitcase, already packed, was in the seminary vestibule, when the rector had me summoned to his
office, that bare cell with whitewashed walls where only two
dark patches were distinguishable: the ebony crucifix above
his table and the rector's cassock, which he wore fitted to his
skeleton body like the sheath of a carbine.

"It is not only your last vacation," he told me, tilting his
head with his habitual gesture, "but these will be your last
days in the world. Do not be alarmed by the somewhat fu-
nereal character of these words. On the contrary, I urge you
to enjoy yourself. Go to parties and meetings; have contacts
with women, without fear; talk to your friends, live a normal

life. You must know beforehand what it is you are renouncing, instead of knowing it when it is too late to back out. Have I expressed myself clearly?"

"Yes, sir," I answered without thinking.

"I am asking you to live, which will prove more difficult than you imagine."

In Zinapécuaro, I did no more perhaps than raise the edge of the curtain and glimpse something of what was going on beyond the window. It was a trivial stroke, a detail without importance for other eyes that were not, like mine, accustomed for years to the confining atmosphere of the seminary and to the unvarying parade of cassocks which my teachers and companions wore.

I followed the rector's recommendations and visited my friends' homes, I held long rambling conversations, I let myself be taken to dinners and outings in the country—almost always organized in my honor—with the result that I felt protected and secure everywhere. I lived in the world and outside the world, perhaps because I was marked, and this mark made the good people look on me as invested with supernatural powers, and the malicious people, as invested with limitations incompatible with those powers, and thus, for one or the other, I was an angel or a hypocrite, and there was no middle ground, or any opportunity of living the normal life advised by the rector, until one day my security collapsed and I understood what he had wanted to tell me.

It happened at a picnic. There were nine of us. Four friends, four women, and I. Oddly enough, two of them had married old companions of mine among those whom the religious persecution had frightened off, and the other two were unmarried. None of them was beautiful. They had the freshness of youth, and the married women distinguished themselves by having achieved a vital fullness which the unmarried women lacked.

We ate on the bank of a stream, in the shadow of the pines, sitting on the grass. In the distance the blue and violet transparencies of the mountains played with the green skin of the nearby woods. One of the men who had brought his camera undertook to take our picture. He arranged the group himself: the women in front, the men behind, myself in the middle. While the photographer advanced and retreated, making all kinds of suggestions, I sought the shadow which one head projected in order to protect myself from the sun, and as I looked toward the front, I observed that the invisible down of the women, on their bare arms, their neck and cheeks, was illuminated and surrounded them like a halo, covering them with its natural clothing, and this clothing was so delicate and so violent, so sweet and so full of animality, that I felt a chill. It revealed the woman, and I understood the dangers which that revelation held in store. The down was the flesh offered as a halo, and I was afraid. Turning my eyes toward the sun, I began to pray: *"Circumdederunt me gemitus mortis, dolores inferni circumdederunt me; et in tribulatione mea invocavi Dominum, et exaudivit de templo sancto suo vocem meam."*

The prayer calmed me. Nevertheless, something had changed within me. The enemy had broken her rhetorical cocoon and was showing her delightful, horribly provocative face, making me understand that I had been living away from the real world and that for the first time I was no different from the one surrounding me.

The return in the cart was a torture. Fog flowed over the mountains, ceaselessly blowing its cottony flakes onto the road. We saw the pine trees as soft masses slightly orange in color, and the sun, almost hidden, swam in a sea of green ground glass.

It was cold. The fog enveloped the wheels and the horses' hooves. The occupants of the cart felt as though they were floating on that soft material and they sought the heat of their bodies, but I tried to remain isolated and did not stop praying for a moment.

On the following day I cut short my vacation. Three months later I was ordained in the cathedral in Morelia, and

when the archbishop from Mexico City pronounced the sacra-
mental formula: "You are still free, but if you wish to embrace the priesthood, take one step forward," I took it resolutely, with an inner feeling in which joy and gratitude were
blended. I was a wretch to whom a great undeserved power
had been given, and this belief ended by blotting out that
light which the image of the world, the flesh, and the devil
had revealed to me in a dazzling apparition.

9

A few days after my ordination I was appointed choirmaster.
Although I had, as I believed at that time, an inborn inclina-
tion toward music and had dreamed of becoming a good or-
ganist, the abbot put me in charge of forming a children's
choir, and little by little I found I was imperceptibly abandoning my old organ of asthmatic, whiny voices and taking
pleasure in my new task.

The houses of our parishioners that I visited mornings and
afternoons immediately furnished me with a good number
of aspiring singers, which the children of our parish catechism
class later reinforced. Many of them came barefoot and
dressed in rags, and there were many who learned the notes
more quickly than the words. In the beginning they showed
much timidity, a distrust growing out of old vexations, but
after two or three weeks their lack of confidence had disappeared, and they applied themselves to studying with that
brilliant, enthusiastic intelligence village children have when
a creative opportunity is offered them.

Six months later we were already giving our first concert
in the cathedral. The thirty children in their red, wide-
sleeved gowns and their starched surplices were facing me,
their eyes fastened on their music sheets, their throats trembling, as if the angels of the heavenly choir had come to life
in the soft dark skins and large eyes of those little ones who,

the night before, had been running about the streets like vagabonds.

There was not one false note, one mistake, one dissonance in their voices. Their pure unalloyed gold, the momentum and joy of their production confirmed in me the idea— perhaps excessively ambitious—that my destiny would be to perfect them, remember their registers and variations, and make of them, of that incomparable tremor in which inno- cence shone through, the ideal instrument for praising our Redeemer.

In the free periods that choir work left me, I explored the very complete cathedral records. Sitting at a table whose feet were carved in the double-headed Austrian eagle, sur- rounded by parchments, I had the feeling of penetrating into a virgin past, into a world peopled by rumors and signs which was revealing its secrets to me when I merely took down a book from the crowded shelves. Before the year was out, I had unearthed some political writings of your predecessor in office, Señor Abad y Queipo, which established the intel- lectual climate that was in vogue in the diocese on the eve of Independence, plus a high mass and two motets composed by eighteenth-century Mexican masters.

These discoveries and the success which the children's choir was achieving turned me into a local celebrity. I granted interviews to people sent by the newspapers and received frequent invitations from aristocratic gentlemen and from religious organizations, which I invariably refused. My voca- tion for musical art and for historical investigation had found its proper channel, and as I progressed, both difficulties and accomplishments restricted me in such a way that I lived secluded in my ivory tower, going from the choir to the parchments without having the slightest idea of what was taking place beyond the iron grillwork of the atrium.

It was written (and it could not be otherwise) that I was to enter the active priesthood. One day, without prior warn- ing, without any preparation, when class had ended and the children were leaving, the abbot appeared and said to me:

"Father, you have been appointed vicar at Pénjamo."

"But—," I managed to stutter.

"There's no but about it," the abbot added dryly. "It's an order from His Grace."

Overcome, I sat down in a choir stall. I was a soft animal, exposed to the dangers of the outside world, and the cathedral was my shell, my home, my protection, and as it happens in the hour of farewell, I never saw it more beautiful than it was that noon. The sun, entering through the windows of the cupola, fell in shafts onto the choir, usually plunged in shadow, and made the candelabras with their iron forged in China reflect the oriental design of the inlaid stalls. The dragons painted on the organ mouths and the thick square notes in the books lying on the raised desk smiled mockingly at me. I should have to forget all that. Why protest? Why rebel? Had I the right to discover motets and direct the choir when religious persecution had exterminated the priests and thousands of souls were dying deprived of spiritual aid?

I fell on my knees in the deserted choir and cried out from the depths of my heart, "My Lord and my God," not knowing that, many years later when I was already old, I was going to pronounce those same words with my soul troubled by other cruel anxieties.

10

No one was waiting for me at the station in Pénjamo. I had just turned twenty-eight, and I felt alone in that world surrounded by peasants and office workers who were getting on and off the trains, busy with their own affairs.

My appearance must not have been very respectable. At the eleventh hour a tailor in Morelia had made me a black suit which was too big for me. The neckband, on the other hand, was too tight, and to top it off, one of my uncles had undertaken to present me with a Panama hat, an old family article already somewhat yellowed, which came down to my ears and contrasted painfully with the rest of my apparel.

I stood on the platform for a while, then, without thinking more about it, picked up my old suitcase, turned my back on the station, and with a light step went to find the town, thus beginning a long, stirring period in my life. There were only two of us priests to attend to the religious needs of eighty thousand inhabitants scattered here and there over an immense territory. The times were far from being tranquil, for if it was indeed true that the flames of religious persecution were being put out, the enmities of the agrarian struggle, on the other hand, were being kindled. The landowners, who had drained the peasants mercilessly for centuries, were now talking of justice and trying to defend their lands, guns in hand, while at the same time the former slaves were engaged in taking it away by violence, since it seems that man has not yet invented a peaceful method of distributing the world's riches more equitably. My heart was naturally with the campesinos, but in Mexico they think that a priest, merely by his being one, must be on the side of the privileged classes, and the local officials hated me even before they took the trouble to find out what my true feelings were.

Your Grace will remember the elderly tithe-collector who was kidnapped in 1934. When I went into the parish office one night, I found on my table a letter from the kidnappers—an unknown man had brought it—in which they were demanding ten thousand pesos for his ransom. That same night I went all over the town knocking at every door. My reading of the letter affected the townspeople. Some handed their savings over to me; others sold their cows and pigs; even the rich dug up their pots full of heavy pesos and gave something, but this immense sacrifice was useless. Three days later, with the money already collected, a peasant found the only trace of the poor priest, his broken, blood-stained glasses, in a cornfield. In that tragic farce when they murdered in the name of the revolution or in the name of Christ, it was up to us to play the role of victims, knowing beforehand that on the following day the fanatics might murder or cut off the ears of the rural teachers, accusing them of being atheists and socialists.

A madness, a hate, a desire to destroy had taken hold of people. The campesinos, the artisans, the businessmen might lack shoes and have only a handful of tortillas to eat, but they were never without a pistol, that dull or shiny pistol which hung bulkily at their side and formed an indispensable part of their body, was their pride, their *raison d'être*. They slept with it under their pillow, they took better care of it than they did of their wives or children, and they preferred to suffer privations, even to die from an illness, rather than to think of the ignominy of selling it.

Does Your Grace ask me if these men were Catholics? I must answer affirmatively. They wore medals of Christ sewn onto their hat brims, blessed medals and scapularies hung around their neck, they went to mass on Sunday, they observed the feast days, and the mere thought of dying unconfessed made their hair stand on end, all of which did not prevent them from regarding their religion as one thing and the not-unlikely possibility of liquidating their enemies as something very different.

Flocks of buzzards soared over the mountains, attracted by the smell of corpses, and the stones on the road were painted with crosses indicating the place where a murdered man had fallen. I cannot put from my memory those crosses or those two beams which rose in the abandoned fields following the passage of death. Even asleep I would see them, and I feared many times I was losing my mind. In the pulpit, in the confessional, in their houses, I never tired of preaching to them, of begging them, of crying out to them, "Thou shalt not kill, thou shalt not spill the blood of thy neighbor," but no one listened to my advice, Monsignor, no one resigned himself to listen to my entreaties or to get rid of his murder weapon, and for an unknown crime that was expiated by the sacrifice of thousands of innocent men, blood continued to saturate the land of Mexico so that it might yield its harvest of crosses painted on the stones.

II

As might be expected, disturbances took place frequently. One morning I met three armed agrarian supporters on the road. They were riding in a compact group, proud of their strength. Seeing me, one of them, a certain lean young man with a blond moustache and faded blue eyes—one of those mementos that white property owners leave in the countryside—threw away the cigar he was smoking and said in the most insolent manner possible:

"Here's the crow. The bad-luck bird."

They played out their comedy. The second, a fat, very dirty man with a long moustache, recited his part:

"Little priest," he said, dragging his words out in the Bajío speech, "come cut off our ears if you're as brave as they say."

I coolly considered the situation. I could ride my horse at the fat one (his spongy cheeks were visibly trembling), take the young punk by the neck (he would not offer any serious resistance), and attack the third man, taking advantage of his surprise. The feat was not only easy, but tempting. Nevertheless, I immediately felt my anger draining away, and I did not answer a word.

Plucking up his courage from my silence, the fat one took out his pistol.

"We ought to give the little priest a lesson he'll never forget," he proposed.

Shouting, the three emptied their guns into the ground, my horse reared up and, although I managed to control it, my breviary fell out during the struggle, and the stamps that I always keep between its leaves were scattered on the ground.

I got down from the horse, picked up my breviary and the stamps, cleaning the dust from them with my sleeve and, without hurrying or turning my head, mounted again, applied my spurs, and rode away from the place. Half an hour later a horseman at full gallop caught up with me. He stopped his foam-covered horse and, removing his hat, said to me:

"Father, three men have been wounded in a scuffle two kilometers from here, and they beg you to confess them."

I turned back and found the three, off the road, lying in the shade of a tree. The fat one—his cheeks sagged in a pitiful manner—kissed my hand and said mournfully:

"Forgive me, father. Our Lord has punished us."

Yes, I must continually remind myself: God was merciful to me. My father's prayer, that imperceptible murmuring that had descended over me in Zinapécuaro brought me safe and sound out of innumerable trials, one more of which I should like to mention because it is characteristic of that era of violence.

One certain night they told me of a man on a distant ranch who was dying. I saddled my horse and began the long journey by the light of an oil lantern. A woman whose head was covered with a shawl stood before the door, and clutching my arm, she begged:

"Wait here, father. I'm going to see if he has the gun."

She returned in a short while, sorrowfully.

"Yes, he still has it in his hand, and he's dying. What can we do?"

I broke away from her gently and opened the door. A man was lying sprawled on a makeshift bunk. In his bony face, under the prominent brows, shone his bloodshot eyes; his mass of hair was like the plumage of a dead bird, and in his right hand he held a nickeled pistol. As he saw me, he made a gesture of shooting and cried:

"Get out of here!"

A convulsion obliged him to let go of the weapon.

"Why such a fuss?" I asked him, approaching.

"Get out of here," he cried again, less forcefully.

He was dying. A bullet had shattered his elbow, and it was filled with pus to the marrow. His dry skin seemed to be burning, and he gave off a sweet, sickening odor.

"Repent of your sins and trust in God. Now you see how simple it is," I added, taking my stole and the little bottle of holy oil from my satchel.

As I finished annointing him, his burning hand sought mine and squeezed it delicately. I went out fighting back tears. Outside stretched the oppressive Mexican night, the deathly silence that weighs heavily on our hearts. I had saved a soul, but I could not rescue the thousands who were dying every day. I was a fisherman who had been given, as his only inheritance, a net full of holes, and through them their souls escaped me, were inevitably drained away, and I could count myself happy if, after spreading it once in a while, one fish remained in its torn meshes at the end of a long exhausting day.

12

Fortunately, weariness prevented me from philosophizing about these matters. From town to town and from ranch to ranch I said mass, baptized, helped the sick, buried the dead. My work began in the early morning, at first light, and ended well after dark. I slept on a mat and ate hard tortillas, a potful of corn liquor, and now and then a bit of roast meat.

I lived in the greatest poverty. I followed Saint Paul's maxim—that he who serves at the altar must eat from the altar—and I charged, I charged for masses, baptisms, weddings, and funerals, but many times I would lack the necessities. The coins that came into one pocket went out the other, and the priest at Pénjamo was obliged to help me a little, unwillingly, and he was scandalized at what he called my prodigality, although he knew very well—and Your Grace is not unaware of it—that it is impossible for a Christian spirit to travel our countryside, face hunger, and have any money at his disposal. Mexican hunger is not spectacular like death, but a sad anxiety, an endless uneasiness in which the pigs, dogs, and chickens share. Nothing special. Only that uneasiness, and those hard beaks, and those mouths equipped with teeth and fangs that root in the earth and in the garbage for something they never find. The rest did not matter—the muddy water, tallow candles, mosquitos, fleas, rags.

There was more, much more than all of that. The poor man feels no attachment to life and tries to escape from his pain through the door of drunkenness and violence. I ought to mention the shouts of drunken men insulting their wives, the broken weeping of their children, and the feeling of impotence that came over me when I took communion to their huts. It is wonderful, I used to tell myself, how the Lord enters into us and establishes his comforting kingdom in the midst of that repugnant atmosphere where children with swollen bellies crawl on the ground while their mother, consumed by fever, receives transfigured the body of Jesus, while the witch doctor waits outside with his potions and his devilish ointments, and I am powerless to deny him entrance because they did not teach us medicine in the seminary, and I can do nothing to save this dying woman.

I ought, Monsignor, to mention other things, to allude to the experiences of my twenty years in the priesthood, except that I am afraid of digressing from the main business and turning this report into an endless catalogue of horrors.

13

I did not experience this painful reality in its raw state, but was protected by an armor plate of dreams, of inner problems, and of reading. Like the marsh birds, my plumage, annointed with learned oils, allowed me to plunge into stagnant water without getting wet, or to fly very high and contemplate things from above, at a great distance, because distance—and I speak as a mountain man—is the only means of making our countryside bearable, of transforming its heavy gloom, its reality of stone, cactus, and prickly pear, its immovable, tragic forms into a music in which harmonies from heaven sing of the redemption and transformation of our desert.

At the beginning of my priesthood, I would just read my breviary or daydream while the mountains of the Bajío filed past me. Later, when I learned to ride, I would loosen the horse's reins and, protected by an umbrella, deliver myself up to the vice of unlimited reading. It was not like sitting in a library, peacefully, sometimes reading, sometimes meditating and taking notes, but it was the satisfaction of a habit, of a morbid need, to such an extent that sometimes the horse would halt of its own accord in a little town plaza or among the huts in a hamlet, and I would remain absorbed in reading, my head full of stories, without becoming aware of the astonished people who surrounded me.

In twenty years I devoured an amazing quantity of books and music scores. I learned to identify the rock layers, the habits of animals, and the organic processes of plants. On clear nights, the luminous outline of the Milky Way was broken by dark fissures, by the soft tissue of the nebula in Orion, the limpid shine of Jupiter, the radiance from blue stars and red stars, from stars that wink and make faces at us, from the throbbing center of the galaxy—the spectacle, in short, of the old sky forever new (who notices the death of a star when millions are burning up and transforming the inert material of space into light?) attracted me with the fascination of an abyss.

In that bit of universe I divined the part of a great whole, the key of a disturbing secret I could not decipher, fearing that my faith would be destroyed and the sole support of my existence would be dashed into nothing.

14

In 1956, exactly three years ago, Your Grace deemed it wise to appoint me priest at Tajimaroa. Bad roads had ground my bones, and I thought with relief that the moment of having a bit of sedentary life had arrived for this wandering priest, nearly fifty years old.

Tajimaroa lies in a narrow valley, so narrow that it might almost merit the name of gully. Although the woodlands extend above it—not abruptly, but in a solemn, majestic manner, with broad stretches of green areas, with substantial clearings where villages and the symmetry of cornfields are outlined—it is possible in a way to speak of an invasion, of an excess, of a grandiose beauty which descends upon us with the violence of a glory, reducing the little village roofs to nothing.

The church, as Your Grace will recall, is a rough construction dating from the sixteenth century; that is, a tall stone cube crowned with merlons similar throughout to those the Franciscans built during the early years of the conquest. But here the builder monk must have been an apprentice, a mere amateur at best, because, fearful that one day his tall stone cube might collapse onto the heads of the faithful, he surrounded it everywhere with gigantic buttresses—that of the apse turned out to be particularly absurd—so that the church, in spite of its fortresslike character, gives the effect of a monstrous invalid supported by enormous crutches.

Even with its deformities and its bizarre orthopedic appliances, the church is not devoid of charm. Time and rain have blackened its stones, casting over the buttresses a rich tapestry of reddish oxidations and thick lichens that has the softness and the tones of old velvet.

The cloister leaning against the church, which serves me as home and office, is thickset, its columns not graceful; the dark rooms smell of dampness, these being things that do not displease me, for I am a little mouse that prefers to live among the ruins, not in modern houses or in those churches where sneezes resound like cannon shot and where Jesus seems to suffer more from the architect's sins than from ours.

An extensive garden of venerable old trees that groan on windy nights like the masts and spars of a ship surrounds church and cloister and completes the perimeter of the church grounds.

I do not possess the leisure to travel over my widespread dominions, and only rarely after mass do I show my face to the town. It is a village, a large town of potholed streets and brick houses. The concrete work—a heavy balcony, a marquee, or the monument to Hidalgo—here and there casts its ugly blotch on the dilapidated, tranquilizing ensemble.

At seven o'clock the stores and artisans' workshops open, brooms undertake (uselessly, of course) to remove the dust, children run to school carrying their satchels, and the fog which the sun turns to gold disguises the potter's field and the uneven stones of the streets through which a smell of bread, leather, and new-cut wood is wafted.

The owners of the chief businesses located on the plaza are little monarchs. Weighed down with children and grandchildren, they are resolved not to give up their commercial thrones, and they can be seen bent like hooks, sitting behind their counters, watching everything above their blurred glasses or, standing, scissors in hand, cutting bright-colored cloth, breathing hard and perspiring, since that privileged class is divided into very weak or very fat old men and there is no possibility of finding an average between them.

All the liveliness is concentrated in the marketplace, which is full of shouting and smoke. The cattle are steaming from head to foot, as are the barbecues sprinkled with salt and wrapped in maguey leaves, the pots of tamales, the corn liquor and chocolate, and the bulls' heads just out of the oven with their horns gilded by the fire and their white eyes that are the specialty of Tajimaroa.

Without any doubt, the best and the worst of my parishioners congregate in the marketplace. These butchers with sharp, bright eyes who work beside mountains of bloody meat, or these harpies with their heads wrapped in their faded shawls, and these maté sellers, half witch, half Gorgon, who enter the houses to gossip at any hour, inventing fantastic stories or taking part in extraordinary fights—if they do indeed make a lot of work, I must confess to Your Grace that my heart is with them and not with the old plaza merchants. Those are tyrannical, ambitious men, although clothed in false meekness, and their longing to possess is projected onto their daughters, whom they would like to have under their jealous, authoritarian thumbs for the rest of their lives. After maintaining a secret engagement fraught with perils, the girl will speak of the possibility of marriage, and then the old man turns his back, his face contracted, and confines himself to saying the dreaded words:

"Daughter, I thought you were going to stay with me all your life."

The men in the marketplace lack that sort of complication. They are elemental beings who revenge themselves for their lack of opportunities, taking and leaving women unscrupulously, getting drunk or quarreling in savage fashion, as if an urge toward destruction is throbbing at the bottom of their primitive consciences.

In this world of virgin passions, the women always carry the heaviest burden. Deprived of liberty and of the men's forthright outlets, almost always abandoned, they must meekly face reality. Here there are some surprises. That prematurely old woman who is happily talking, squatting behind her kettle, has got up at two o'clock in the morning to make tamales and has come to the market at five. Her tamales sold, she will prepare a meal for her husband, who is a lazy drunkard, and at seven o'clock in the evening she will sit on the edge of the sidewalk waiting for them to throw her husband out of the cantina, as a bundle is thrown out, which invariably happens every day in the year. She is there, whether it is cold or raining or thundering, until the man revives and she can take him off to bed.

I advise her:

"Let him lie there. Let him come to, woman. You're supporting the wretch by your work, and yet he beats you. Have you no pity for yourself?"

"Ah, señor cura," she replies, "this is my cross, and I must bear it joyfully."

Her neighbor, that woman over there who wraps her face, proud and withered as if carved on a piece of dark wood, in a black shawl, has seen her only two daughters ruined. Tired of playing, those two have returned to their mother's house with their children, and she must support all of them by selling shoes and ribbons amidst the flies and mud of the marketplace.

They never complain. They do not like to speak of their affairs. If they are insulted, they answer with insults, but if they hear a compassionate word, if they are aware of the slightest friendly sign, these women will bow their heads in shame, cover their faces with their shawl, and only their shoulders, shaking convulsively, tell us that they are bursting into tears.

15

Your Grace was speaking of the docility of my parishioners. Certainly they are docile, even too docile. They accept work and pain with a passive, almost stoic disdain which makes them invulnerable. Nevertheless, behind that protective covering, that resignation with which they accept their destiny, those eyes cloudy with enigmas, are hidden an unhealthy

sensitivity, a magic feeling for life, and a reservoir of rebelliousness capable of exploding in a second with astonishing violence.

They believe blindly in the efficacy of amulets, in prophecies, in hidden treasures, in miracles, and in supernatural
apparitions, and I often anxiously wonder whether the responsibility of fostering these superstitions does not fall upon
us. Without going further, last month our missionary bulletin published Sister Lucía's prophecy about the darkness
which will inexorably fall upon the world in 1960. I did not
consider it of any importance. The destruction which has
threatened mankind since 1945 has unleashed a wave of mys-
tics and visionaries who are busy announcing universal ca-
tastrophes, and while the prophecy of this naïve survivor of
of the Fátima group had the moral support of the Portuguese
bishops and our own, I expected that the announcement
would pass unnoticed.

Two days later, the announcement of the prophecy did
have its effect, and thousands of parishioners invaded the
church carrying handfuls of candles smelling of honey,
matches, and bundles of pinewood resin to be blessed. I
ordered the doors of the baptistry opened, and in the company of my vicars, I stayed there for several hours, swinging
the censer, sprinkling plenty of holy water onto those fragile
objects, investing them with the supernatural powers with
which the devout have for centuries been able to conjure
away epidemics, floods, and storms.

As money filled the trays and poor boxes, time retreated,
and only animal terror remained, the fear that prevailed in
feudal days, the magic conception of the universe in which
phenomena can be modified and twisted and eternal laws
replaced by the delirious prophecy of a poor sick woman.
I saw the grave faces of my parishioners, their humble faces
to which a new worry had been added, and I felt tempted
to go up into the pulpit and tell them:

"Sister Lucía is mad! The Portuguese bishops and the publishers of the parish bulletin are mad. Do not be afraid. The sun, our sun, is a star, not too small and not too large, but it is a good, reasonable star that for ten thousand millions of years has preserved a wonderful balance between the force of its gravity and the resilient force of its gases.

"Everything that refers to the sun is extraordinary. Its dimensions, its age, the secret of its energy would be outside our human age, our measurements, our conception of relativity, if we did not resort to mathematical formulas. Only these could speak to us, in their coded, precise language, of the strange phenomena which operate on the sun; of a heat and density which increase from the outside toward the center until they reach temperatures, pressures, and densities which in their turn start complex thermonuclear reactions. There, in the innermost part of the star, atoms have lost their electrons and are nothing but nuclei, heavy nuclei onto which the swift protons strike, making them explode, creating a new energy out of them, a photon, a gamma ray of very short wave length, and this proton in its travels across the solar beds keeps colliding with other nuclei and increasing its wave length and becoming transformed into the wave train, into the electromagnetic current which man for several millennia has called light and heat in different languages.

"The gamma ray, the photon, my beloved brothers in our Lord Jesus Christ, does not wholly explain the secret of solar energy. At the same time that protons disintegrate their nuclei, another conversion is going on, that of hydrogen into helium, the ever-present carbon cycle which permits the sun to nourish itself and to create energies in the live laboratories of its interior to assure it another ten thousand million years without diminishing its brilliance, without decay, without loss of its prodigious vitality, because it is a lamp supplied with precious fuel, a cosmic force too great for Atlas's shoulders or the Hindu tortoise's shell, a star God created

intending it to remain lighted, and lighted it shall remain
for thousands of centuries after your grandchildren and the
grandchildren of their grandchildren have disappeared.

"This is my prophecy. Between it and that of Sister Lucía
there is only a difference of time. What she announced for
1960, I announce for another date, at hand or far off, according to how we measure with our own or with astro-
nomical measuring instruments. So you may go calmly back
to your houses and keep your candles, matches, and pine
branches against the day when our old planet of light may
suffer one of its usual disruptions and dark shadows descend
upon Tajimaroa. Thanks be to God."

The phrases of my sermon were arranging themselves in
my mind while I was observing their serious, worried faces
reflected in the vast bowl of the baptismal font. It was useless to try to tell them the truth. Their eyes saw the blinding
flames of the Mexican sun, but they did not see its granular
skin, its spots, its rays, its storms. It was useless to speak to
them of the carbon cycle, of gamma rays, of the sun in its
old age transformed into a red giant, of its final destiny as
a white dwarf lost in the intense life of the galaxy.

16

They filed out of the church and looked timidly at the sun.
Beside them our sacristan, a lame old man, skipped obsequi-
ously, looking for additional alms. He had been the most
fervent spreader of the prophecy, and the atmosphere of fear
and mystery created by the forecast of darkness had transformed him into an excited, happy man because his deplorable lameness was evidence of a miracle that had taken place
forty years ago in Tajimaroa, and he enjoyed the opportunity
of telling about it and of showing everyone his thank-offer-
ing hanging on a wall of the sacristy, where an anonymous
painter had left a record of this incredible event.

In the year 1920 the future sacristan was a young artisan who spent his money (and often someone else's) on getting drunk every day. He drank bad wine. He could be seen in the cantinas, a glass in his hand, his clothing dirty, his hair mussed, his eyes casting sparks of fire. A dense, almost liquid air surrounded him, like an atmosphere of his own, in which floated not only a large number of knives, razors, and metal pins, but also (though they were invisible) toads, snakes, and diabolical little monsters which issued continually from his mouth without his being aware of it.

His mother, a pious old woman, dogged her son's footsteps in vain, begging him by all the saints to change his way of life. The future sacristan did not understand either entreaties or prayers. They measured him with the purple tape of San Benito so that he might die or be redeemed; they tried to expel his demons by means of exorcisms; they made supplications and novenas—to no avail. Instead of being reformed, the young man carried his bad conduct to extremes —if this were possible—and one night he lost his head and beat his mother, the neighbors came in, and the police carted him off to jail.

At two o'clock in the morning, the prisoners sleeping in their cells were rudely awakened by the young man's shouts.

"Help!" he exclaimed, beside himself. "Help! The devil has got me! He's taking me to hell!"

The scene that presented itself to the prisoners justified the future sacristan's fear. In the weakly lighted courtyard a gigantic bird had gripped him in its claws and had already lifted him fifteen or twenty feet when the prisoners, recovering from their astonishment, began to sing the *Alabado* hymn.

At that moment the devil, fatally wounded, released his prisoner, the young man fell to the ground, breaking his leg, and the bird, croaking lugubriously this time, disappeared among the night shadows.

My sacristan's lameness, that authentic proof of an antici-

pated divine justice, was introduced into our world in a natural manner; it was consistent with the portents that governed his life; it was part of a great indivisible whole which
I could fight only at the risk of wearing us all out. To banish
mystery from their souls, to cure them of their fear was
equivalent to losing them, to changing them, to killing in
them a faith I might not be able to replace with any other
counsel, and I kept silent.

Only the formulas remained. The medieval Latin formula,
the old formula which had not suffered attrition in spite
of the centuries gone by: *Ne despicias omnipotens Deus,
populum tuum in afflictione clamantem: sed propter gloriam
nominis tui, tribulatis sucurre placatus;* and the formula
written in a coded language, the law of matter established
by an Old Testament man: Energy equals mass times the
velocity of light squared.

Yes, Monsignor, only those two formulas were left. The
old one, the one that governed our world (I mean the little
world of Tajimaroa), the key that opened the gates of hope
with its sacrosanct power, and the law of physical matter,
the revealed secret of the universe which the devil has transformed into a prophecy of darkness and death, against which
neither exorcisms nor resins nor matches nor blessed wax
candles are of any avail.

17

On the very day of my arrival, I found out that the town
had a master. He lived in a house built on the other side of
the highway away from the center of Tajimaroa. This removal was a rather fictitious one, for his name sounded re-
peatedly, and he made his presence strongly felt in the far-
thest corners.

From the beginning they advised me of the propriety of
visiting him. My predecessor, the priest to whom Your Grace

referred in our conversation, had maintained affectionate relations with him which had surely helped him to preserve the tranquility of the parish, and I must not ignore the elemental fact that I could do nothing without gaining the good will of that all-powerful man.

Ulises Roca—Don Ulises, as everyone called him—was not the mayor, or the local deputy, or the owner of the principal sawmills, or even the richest man in town. He was above those considerations, and his power, like that of kings, emanated from a higher order hidden from the eyes of simple mortals.

My arrival did not pass unnoticed by Don Ulises. His wife, Doña Paula, saw me in the sacristy after my first Sunday mass. She is an elderly woman—she must be about seventy—and although she keeps her distance from her neighbors, she does it not from pride, but rather from fear of contracting unnecessary obligations. She kissed my hand, bade me welcome, and left without inviting me to visit her, without saying a word about her husband.

I preferred to let affairs progress slowly. The master of the town could stay in his house, I in mine, and God in everybody's. Three days later I came upon him accidentally. I was in my jeep en route to a mountain village, and he was driving a red pickup truck, accompanied by his bodyguard. His gray eyes regarded me with a certain curiosity, and he slipped me a salute, touching the brim of his ten-gallon hat with the tip of his fingers.

Doña Paula continued to attend church, sometimes in the company of her daughter María and her young daughter-in-law, but she would leave quickly as soon as mass was over, without saying a word to me. The townspeople, on the other hand, never stopped referring to the "boss." They carried him within themselves, and for them he was an obsession, a fixed idea that wholly dominated them.

They would be telling me of their troubles or their sorrows, and immediately his name would crop up. Don Ulises dominated their past, present, and future, and nothing official occurred in their business or in their domestic conflicts that did not bear a strict relation to that personage whom I soon became accustomed to regard as the *deus ex machina*. Even on the ground of moral conflicts, which was mine, people preferred to consult him in matters of conscience. He intervened in their quarrels, and he offered solutions to their problems which, as Your Grace may imagine, were not always reconciled with Christian principles.

At the end of two weeks this embarrassing situation took a turn which I would venture to describe as dramatic, had not the circumstances of my former life worn down that adjective until it ceased to have any meaning.

One night I was preparing to dine, when an old man presented himself in the dining room and, with his usual timidity and reticence, told me of a sick man who needed confession.

"Who is the sick man?" I asked him. One of my vicars could go.

"The sick man is my son. Actually," he added after a slight hesitation, "he's not ill, he's wounded, and he wants you to confess him."

I pictured the scene that awaited me: the young man, wounded in one kidney from which the blood was flowing, was trying to avoid the police.

"Let's go," I told him, getting up from the table.

The old man made a gesture to stop me.

"Doesn't it matter to you, señor cura, that the house is watched by the police?"

"Why should that bother me?"

"The boss's bodyguard wounded him, and perhaps you may become a suspect . . ."

"Say no more," I interrupted him. "This is my duty."

The old man's house was in an outlying neighborhood, under surveillance by two policemen. The youth was lying on a bed covered with a mattress made of pieces of varicolored cloth, with his arm in a plaster cast. Because of the bandage over his face, only his mouth with its swollen lips and one eye that looked out through puffed lids were visible.

That night I limited myself to confessing him. Later, during his prolonged convalescence, I visited him frequently, and in those immobilized days he told me his story, a story to which I listened with particular interest because it reflected, without distortions, the image of the "boss's" power, that is, the image, as I discovered with terror, of my own parish.

18

Manuel Espino, the only son of the little old man (a retired former treasury employee), was studying medicine in Morelia, supporting himself by odd jobs and a scholarship of fifty pesos per month which the Colegio de San Nicolás had granted him.

He was characterized by his passionate temperament. A vehemence, an inner fire which made him known by communicating itself to others, lighted up his dark eyes. If an idea took hold of him, he would speak quickly, riding roughshod over it; his delicate nose would contract, losing color; his fists would clench; and a lock of hair fall over his forehead. Born in 1936, when the boss's rule was already established, he hated that kind of subjection and spent a large part of his time reading and becoming practiced in what he called, not without adopting an air of mystery, the *"coup d'état."*

During his vacations and sometimes on weekends he would come to Tajimaroa to visit his sweetheart, a girl of his own age named Elena Zúñiga. Elena's father, a diffident little man burdened with children, supported himself precariously by doing accounts for four or five stores and shops and arranging matters of wills and taxes. Her mother, a woman who was old before her time from childbirth and privations, was of an irascible nature, and her bitter unburdenings loudly expressed were often audible in the street.

Elena, to say it with a time-honored expression, "kept up appearances." An intimate friend of María, Don Ulises's older daughter, and of the half-dozen girls on whom rested responsibility for keeping up the local aristocracy's feminine prestige without visible lapses, she was not very different from them. She wore the same hair styles and the same dresses, but the resentful, practiced glances of young ladies who were excluded from the exclusive circle soon revealed—and spread the fact—that her dresses, shoes, and coats, in spite of the necessary alterations, had belonged the year before to her rich friends.

For old Don Ulises, busy with his affairs or his occasional amours, Elena was just one of the many young ladies who visited his home every day, until things changed one day, and behind his daughter's friend appeared the woman. Her green eyes, shadowed by thick black brows, her delicate white skin, and her magnificent chestnut hair began to attract his attention and to acquire a seduction and a charm which were taking hold of the boss.

Don Ulises undertook his new conquest in his own fashion, appointing her father assistant to the city treasurer and accountant for a sawmill on his property which he operated at the rear of his house. With him there was no problem. He was a meticulous, efficient employee, one of those servants who always give more than they receive, without achieving recognition from anyone because of their insignificance and their imploring looks. The boss demanded of him something different besides his work, and when the old man understood at last what was involved, his figure shrank, and the abject glance in his short-sighted, weary eyes became more noticeable.

Trapped, Elena spoke frankly to Manuel:

"I don't want to hide anything from you," she told him. "Don Ulises is pursuing me. He's bought my father by giving him a couple of jobs, and my mother, who's sick and has had a miserable life, is persecuting me with her complaints. 'Pay attention,' she begs me. 'He's a rich man, the boss of the town, and he'll make you happy. Look in my mirror,' she interrupts my excuses in her screaming voice, 'look in my mirror. At your age I was married to that wretch your father, and at forty I look like an old woman of sixty. I've lived cooped up in the kitchen like a slave to all of you, without clothes, without any fun, and now I've lost my life, you understand? I've lost it, and it's too late for everything.' "

"That is what your mother said. What do you say?" asked Manuel.

"I love you, you know that very well, but in my case love is a luxury, something completely outside our reach."

"Do what you like," Manuel replied. "You're free to choose between being the sweetheart of an old boss or the wife of a poor student. I won't give you up. They'd say I was afraid of Don Ulises."

"I understand now, señor cura," Manuel told me, "that my behavior was neither good nor intelligent. Like all of us, Elena was a victim of poverty and despair. I remember her mother very well—her missing teeth, her dirty dress, her eternal bitterness. She yearned for a different destiny for her daughter, and I made the situation more difficult with my stubbornness in visiting her every day, pretending that I was waiting for her at her window as if our relations had not suffered an irreparable break."

After he had stayed two or three hours, Elena began to close the window, overcome by her decision.

"Go," she pleaded. "I beg you to go. Don't make me unhappier than I already am."

"I won't move from here," Manuel replied.

"They'll kill you without reason. You can't fool with Don Ulises."

"The old man is a coward and will send his thugs. You can tell him I'm not afraid of them."

As a matter of fact, Avelino, the commandant of police and executioner of Don Ulises's plans, appeared on one of many such nights, followed by three armed men.

"What are you doing at this house?" Avelino asked.

"What business is it of yours?" asked Manuel defiantly.

"What business of mine, you say? Don't you know I'm the commandant of police?"

"Don't *you* know," Manuel said, putting the accent on the familiar *tú*, "that it's no crime to wait for your fiancée in front of her window?"

"You are getting familiar with me, eh?"

"You called me *tú* first."

Avelino did not know what to reply. The unexpected defiance disturbed him, and his small brain tried vainly to find an adequate reply.

"Did you lose your tongue in the cantina?"

"You're going to lose even your means of walking if you don't leave right now," Avelino exploded, blind with rage.

"Let your cuckolded old boss come to tell me so, if you have any shame left."

In the face of such blasphemy, Avelino retreated as though he had received a blow. Leaning on the ironwork, Manuel observed him coldly. The armed men were a few steps away, their guns in hand.

Manuel understood that if he left the iron railing, he would expose himself to certain death, and he remained there motionless, hoping that Elena would open the window and her presence put the gunmen to flight.

Avelino stepped cautiously forward. Don Ulises, softened by Elena's entreaties, had forbidden him to use a gun, and Manuel was far from being one of those cowardly residents or drunkards whom he still managed to subdue in spite of his fat and his fifty hard-spent years.

As soon as Manuel had him within reach, he aimed a blow above the belly, knocking him to the ground, and tried to flee. The bodyguards corralled him, and an unequal fight began which ended when, as a result of a blow, Manuel's head collided with the ironwork of the window and he lost consciousness. As he was recovering, the gunmen imprisoned his arms, and Avelino was waiting.

"You'll see who I am," he warned. "You asked for it."

Joining both his hands together by interlocking his fingers, he hit him again and again in the face, and when he fell, the gunmen stamped mercilessly upon him.

Roofs, stars, the whole world collapsed on Manuel. He did not feel the kicks. Only that crumbling, those fragments of the world that pressed down on him with their terrible weight. Nearly dying, he uttered a cry and saw Elena's face framed by her disordered hair. The men retreated, and the world, by a strange phenomenon, resumed its former position and surrounded him indifferently.

I already knew what I needed to know about Don Ulises. I did not rush to meet him face to face. I did not defend the harassed sheep which Your Grace had confided to my care when you appointed me priest at Tajimaroa. I too, like Elena, "kept up appearances." I could not go beyond that limit. No political consideration forced me to maintain friendly relations with my parishioners' bully.

19

Don Ulises knew his business very well. At eight o'clock in the morning his truck would leave his house and begin traversing the uneven streets of Tajimaroa. Through its green windows framed in shiny nickel we observed the solemn, proud faces, always the same, of the half-dozen gunmen who made up his entourage. They paraded in a slow, majestic procession, as if they were their own portraits, along past the workshops, the stores, among the women who were coming from mass, the vendors, and the burros laded with fodder and vegetables heading for the market.

The truck entered the plaza, describing a wide circle, and
stopped before the door of the Ayuntamiento. The doors
were opened, the bodyguards got out one by one, not hurrying, and set up a guard around the vehicle, an offensive and
totally unnecessary guard because the people were peaceable
and the wild idea of attacking Don Ulises did not enter anyone's head.

At that moment, as if by magic, the municipal president in
person came out of the dilapidated palace, followed by the
secretary, the treasurer, and the councilmen, carrying papers
and notebooks in their hands, and not concerned for the dignity of their office, they ran toward the truck—Don Ulises
had remained sitting inside—and right there, in view of the
people, they spoke with him, submitting the town accounts
and business to him. They took notes of his decisions and,
fifteen minutes later, the audience having ended, the gunmen returned to their seats, the gendarmes raised their hands
to their caps, and the members of the town council proudly
watched the departure of the large truck that symbolized for
them the power and the glory of their chief.

This daily, almost miraculous apparition—it could travel
as well on a cloud as on a magic carpet—had begun more
than twenty-five years ago as an unvarying ritual in which
only the faces of his bodyguards changed, becoming older
each time, and the automobiles that Don Ulises bought every
year becoming more sumptuous each time.

The young men who saw him go by on his way to the
palace in 1928 in a Ford with three pedals were the fat,
gray-haired men who witnessed, with half-closed eyes from
their workshops and stores, the parade of the 1959 Mercury
truck. The old men died, the houses were filled with new
people, customs changed, governments changed, the word
"democracy" was heard on everyone's lips, but their feudal
lord's parade, the display of his magnificence, continued to
project his stereotyped image onto the unchanging back-

ground of mildewed stones, stained stucco houses, and doors opening onto little inner gardens where ferns spread riotously.

20

In the afternoons Don Ulises would play dominoes. Amidst the smoke that filled the cantina the boss would sit with his back to the wall, and on his right, not in the front row but slightly apart, was outlined the figure of Adalberto, his chief gunman. He wore an immaculate linen shirt and, judging by his stern appearance, his carefully cropped graying moustache, and the bifocal glasses he wore, he might have been taken for a rich old farmer now retired from business.

As the old men of the town tell it, Adalberto was the man at the beginning of the boss's rule who masterminded the coups which the boss launched against town councils and rebellious unions, but age had turned him into Don Ulises's shadow, a respectable, silent shadow above which projected the blustering and the jovial disposition of his boss.

At his left would always sit Arteaga, secretary of the town council and of the peasants' league—both posts he had held uninterruptedly for more than fifteen years, by reason of which they called him the perpetual secretary—a dark, chubby man of about fifty with malicious little eyes and thick, half-open lips which allowed his four eye-teeth capped with gold to show. Arteaga's entrance into Tajimaroa, occurring in 1930, is still remembered. Rural guards brought him in tied hand and foot because of a certain cattle robbery which had taken place in Irimbo, his birthplace, and he faced prosecution until Don Ulises, won over by the cattle thief's ability, eliminated the court proceedings and added him to his little gang. People privately called him "Cow Thief," and they would have given almost anything to be able to say it to his face, had not their fear of his pistol—he had the reputation of being an excellent shot—put a brake on this legitimate desire.

The treasurer, Don Luis G. Bolaños—the "G." belonged to the apostle of his youth, San Luis Gonzaga—was another of the faithful at the daily domino game. Of all that group, he was the only one who wore a suit with a jacket and a tie, a hard collar and a felt hat. He would sit down keeping his knees together and was continually wiping his forehead or noisily blowing his nose with a handkerchief whose corners showed above his jacket pocket. He would nurse his glass of rum in his hand and put it down only when, noisily and triumphantly, he added a domino to the articulated worm that crawled over the table and called out:

"Got you with the fives! You owe me three glasses of rum, Don Ulises."

Of course, he was a ridiculous old man, burdened with unmarried daughters, who loved his rum too well, but no one, not even Don Ulises himself, dared to make fun of him. Don Luis was learned in the science of mathematics. He carried the score of the game in his head without needing to write it down. He could add and subtract large sums in his head, and this knowledge allowed him easily to dominate his opponents in the game and to satisfy the Morelia deputies who reviewed the town council's accounts every year.

The municipal president, Guadalupe Cielo, who occupied the next chair, was the youngest of the group—he had joined the gang in 1950—and the exact opposite of Don Luis. Guadalupe, a slender half-breed of very few words, had dark, almond-shaped eyes, and his distrustful, enigmatic glance made him disagreeable and an object of fear. He hated alcohol, and he never understood the mechanics of the game for the sake of which he sat for long hours without speaking, diffident and tense. After four or five matches he would open his mouth, sigh heavily, and raise his eyes to Don Ulises, looking for help.

"That's enough for today," the boss would say, knocking over the rest of the dominoes.

"I'll never learn to play like Don Luis," the mayor would apologize.

"It doesn't matter," the boss commented. "You know how to fight, just as Don Luis knows how to do accounts."

"What use is it to fight?" asked Don Luis after he emptied his glass. "What good is it to carry that pistol?"

"That pistol serves, among other things," Don Ulises would explain, employing a convincing tone, "so that you may occupy your job as treasurer."

"I don't see the connection, although—," he corrected himself in confusion, "we'd better talk of something else."

The president's face hardened. He was trying to forget some ghosts, but the ghosts returned doggedly to importune him. His Uncle Simón—the only survivor of his family clan —had killed Juan Ramírez, the head of the rival clan, and he was not seen again in Ziraguato. Was he responsible for that death? For that death and the deaths of many people killed before he was born? No, he had avoided them, had tried to pass them unnoticed—he always tried to pass unnoticed—and those were the ones who went looking for him that Sunday morning, the ones who surrounded him treacherously while his shoes were being shined in the plaza at Ziraguato. With a kick he knocked the bootblack's box flying— he was another accomplice of the Ramírezes—and, jumping behind a tree, he fired.

Of that exploit—an exploit which many different novelists have looked into with scant luck—people often used to speak in our province. I do not know the details of the fight, but the fact is that that man, alone and pursued, was able to exterminate all the men of the enemy clan. A few women and a boy of ten—who had already been taught hatred and the handling of weapons in order to avenge his relatives who had fallen in the plaza—were left. He would have to wait . . .

Meanwhile, they jailed Guadalupe Cielo, and Don Ulises saved him from the complicated lawsuit, carrying him off to Tajimaroa and in due course making him his municipal president.

Avelino was at the bar drinking with the rest of the gunmen, police officers, and councilmen whose salary the town council paid. Old or young, they were all united by the prestige of the boss's power, by terror and by a few impudent deeds, the recollection of which the gunmen's continual vexations and the all-powerful presence of weapons kept fresh in mind. The eight or ten men of the entourage—with the exception of the treasurer—displayed their cartridge belts full of bullets, their large pistols that bulked around their waists (the principal topic of conversation was weapons), and if this exhibition of warlike power were not enough to maintain the fictitious peace of Tajimaroa, the truck parked in front of the cantina door displayed a machine gun and two telescopic rifles on its seats, so that these excursions to the taverns or to the Ayuntamiento seemed more like safaris than administrative visits or peaceful domino games.

21

The game over, the men hurried to empty their glasses, getting ready to leave. Don Ulises stopped them, making a gesture as he asked the mayor:

"Well, Guadalupe, what do you intend to do with those two prisoners?"

"You tell me, Don Ulises."

"It's a difficult problem," the boss went on thoughtfully.

"What is this all about? A complicated new story?" the treasurer asked.

"No, it's a really funny story."

"Tell it, tell it, Don Ulises."

Avelino and the gunmen approached the table, and the

barkeeper stopped washing glasses. No sound was heard other than the passing of cars on the highway.

"It's the story of the two woodcutters from the lumber company," Don Ulises began. "On Saturday they cashed their checks and went to a baptism. Was it a baptism or a wedding?"

"It was a baptism," Guadalupe confirmed.

"After the baptism they went on an all-night binge, according to their story, and they remember only that they woke at ten o'clock on Sunday morning in a sort of corral, half dead, without a centavo. One of them said:

" 'Either I must be dreaming, or hunger makes me see visions. Isn't there a lamb here?'

" 'Yes,' replied the other. 'It's the fattest lamb I've ever seen in my life.'

" 'Suppose it's the devil? It's too big to be a lamb.'

" 'We ought to talk to it, but if it's really the devil, he surely won't understand Castilian. They tell me devils understand only Latin and English.'

" 'In the name of God,' said the first drunk, addressing the animal, 'in the name of God I order you to tell me if you're a lamb, or if you're the devil.'

"Frightened by the presence of the intruders, the animal uttered a penetrating bleat.

" 'It bleats,' the second drunk reasoned convincingly. 'Therefore it's not the devil, but a lamb that is saying, "Eat me." '

" 'God is good to us, little brother. Don't ask for more. The barbecue has fallen on us from heaven!'

"Since God had revealed it to them, the two drunks took the animal home and organized a party that lasted the rest of Sunday and all of Monday. On Tuesday things cleared up. The lamb was certainly not the devil, but a twenty-thousand-peso lamb, a Rambouillet with the best pedigree in the world —in a word, the stud animal which the general had given to the town and which the town council was keeping in that specially built corral, with the hope of improving our live-stock."

They were all weeping with laughter. The treasurer wiped his tears with his handkerchief and exclaimed:

"A twenty-thousand-peso barbecue! Not even at Camacho's wedding, Don Ulises, not even at Camacho's wedding."

"Well," said Don Ulises, consulting his watch, "we have laughed enough now. I am leaving."

The session had ended. Avelino went out into the street to wake the driver asleep inside the truck.

Standing up, the men formed a circle around the boss.

"Do you have any orders?" asked the perpetual secretary.

"None. Tomorrow we'll talk in council about those two prisoners."

Accompanied by Adalberto, the boss got into his truck and set off for Santiaguito, a ranch on his property located four kilometers from Tajimaroa.

22

Santiaguito, where Don Ulises kept his young mistress and her two small children, was in fact a forbidden spot. There he spent his nights guarded by Adalberto or another of his trusted gunmen, but aside from them no one was admitted to the farm. His guests were officially received in his house on the highway or at his sulphur baths on the mountain, and if he sometimes took them to Santiaguito, he did so without entering the house, limiting himself to showing them quickly over his fields and stables, somewhat against his will, im-pelled rather by his pride of ownership, as powerful in him as the desire to keep secret his relations with Elena.

Is not this love for earthly things, Monsignor, the charac-teristic feature of one style of American feudalism, that is, the feature most characteristic of those who have managed to

promote themselves in politics and enrich themselves in its
shadow after having suffered innumerable privations?

Don Ulises showed perhaps greater attachment to the goods
of this world than the old-time landowners, who were already
familiar since birth with extensive, wealthy properties. He
would half-close his eyes in a special way when he was trying
to take in one section of his fields planted to wheat; his hand
unconsciously acquired a jealous sensuality when he caressed
a pear or an apple, and when he rode through his fields with
some of his city guests, it was not difficult for him, carried
away by his enthusiasm, to get down from his horse and,
picking up a handful of earth, exclaim:

"All of this I did foot by foot, field by field, as big things
are done." He would look at the dust slipping through his
fingers, and his hoarse voice, breaking, would reveal an emotion which was unusual for him. "I was a woodcutter all my
life. I had eyes only for the pine woods, and I was not interested in the uncultivated lands full of stumps that were left
over. Crossing these waste lands one day, I realized that the
time had come to exchange the axe for the plow, and I began
to buy them up. The old men of the town laughed mali-
ciously. 'Ulises Roca,' they would say, pointing their finger at
their temple, 'has lost his mind. Those highlands full of
boulders and stumps aren't good for anything.' I cleared the
land with tractors and ox teams. I built terraces to prevent
washouts, and I planted them. At first I planted corn and
beans, because people need the essential foods to eat. Then,
contrary to the experts' opinion, I planted wheat, and finally
I planted fruit trees. 'It's not the soil for fruit trees,' the farmers pronounced, and it was not, actually. All my little trees
appeared to have gone crazy. The cherry trees flowered in
July, the pear trees in August; the figs were loaded with figs
that never matured, and the apple trees, those California apple trees I acquired at an exorbitant price, produced fruit
the size of a cherry, and all that without counting the pests,

parasites, and insects that attacked them, devouring them down to the last leaf. I'm stubborn, señor, stubborn as a mule, and I spent years on end spraying them with dust and chemicals, pruning them, spending a fortune on fertilizers and grafts, and now you can see my apples, try my cherries and my figs that are as sweet as those of Normandy or Smyrna. But all of this—corn, wheat, fruit trees—are things of the past. Time always claims its own, and the other day I became aware, with surprise, that Mexico City has had a remarkable growth. What could I furnish that city of five million inhabitants, or rather, what could my lands furnish, located a hundred and fifty kilometers away on a good highway? I decided to find out for myself, and I spent two weeks traveling through the streets, the plazas, the gardens, sticking my nose into houses and shops, sniffing into every corner.

"My curious tendency to consider human beings as animals, which age has transformed into a mania, made me discover many interesting things. No, it is not a question of finding their resemblance to toads or horses or birds, but of observing how they really are; that is, like animals that, in spite of their civilization, their books, their religion, their inventions, do not succeed in hiding or disguising their true condition as animals. I watched them walking along the streets, going into the buildings, shops, markets, and that activity reminded me of the activity of an ant hill. They were all going to work in order to eat (they have drones there, too), and they all carried baskets or packages of food or ate standing on the sidewalks or sitting in the restaurants and inns, but they were forever putting something into their bellies, they were forever moving their jaws, and when they were not devouring something, they were looking at the women. They got excited looking at the women painted on signboards, on theater billboards, in the store windows; they waited for them on corners and in doorways; they went arm-in-arm with them to theaters and movies, to dances, to restaurants, to hotels, and to the special houses or to their own houses. I was astonished at the number of ways in which carnal desire is aroused, disguised, and dissembled in the cities. We provincials—I say it in passing—are more direct in everything, and we don't go about satisfying our animal hunger for bread and women with so many circumlocutions and affectations.

"To eat, to reproduce, to be entertained, to be healed in order to go on eating and reproducing, and finally to die, to die at home or in the street in an unfortunate manner, or to die in a big hospital or in a little sanitorium, to be borne along, to be given a wake, honored and wept over in a rented room at a funeral parlor where the dead are laid out on elegant platforms, on eight or ten floors, where they have a cafeteria and rest rooms, and then to leave there borne on men's shoulders and be dragged again out to the edge of the city, to the city cemeteries, where they remain for years under an artificial stone monument—in Mexico, where there are only natural stones!—these were the principal stages followed by city-dwellers, stages that I reconstructed step by step while I stuffed myself in restaurants or marched in funeral processions behind the coffin of an unknown dead man.

"When the two weeks were up, I returned to my village and made a decision which perhaps may seem odd to you: I would sell flowers. They would not be roses or carnations or chrysanthemums, but another kind of flower they sell on the highways, large beautiful decorative flowers that could be used for a fiesta as well as a wake, flowers without a taboo like gardenias, which 'smell of death,' without thorns like roses, without the fragility of carnations and chrysanthemums, very expensive and much sought-after flowers that I would make rain upon the city at ridiculous prices. A rain of flowers . . . When I was a boy in Veracruz, on the Tuesday of Carnival, people in costumes and passersby would toss flowers for the space of three or four hours; the air was filled with petals, and they called this the 'rain of flowers.' "

Don Ulises was speaking engulfed up to his waist in the

ocean of Dutch gladiolus that surrounded Santiaguito. Along the highway, now invaded by the shadow of the mountains, stretched the sumptuous pink, white, and crimson tapestries of his gardens, and those brilliant patches were not only a novelty in the ancient countryside, but a contrast that redeemed the dark, compact tones of the pine woods and the metallic blues of the distant mountain ranges.

Dozens of campesinos were cutting the stems heavy with newly opened flowers and piling them along the edge of the highway for Don Ulises's trucks to take to Mexico City.

"A rain of flowers . . . will fall on Mexico City tomorrow and will decorate the banquet tables, the weddings in the churches, the houses of the poor and the rich, the coffins of the dead, the cemetery graves . . . They call me boss. Haven't you heard them call me boss? Why don't they call me gladiolus grower? I set up that business; the idea came to me to import millions of Dutch bulbs and plant them in these fields where corn was once cultivated with an Egyptian plow. I was the creator of this wealth, but my enemies say I've enriched myself by robbing the Tajimaroa town council. The poor devils! Do you know how much my gladiolus has brought me every year? Three hundred thousand pesos and in good years, half a million! That is my wealth. Yes, I do get something from my woods, from my sawmills, from my wheat and fruit trees, but it all goes to buy breeding stock and erect buildings for my health resort, because I am thinking of tomorrow and of the tourists who will come to enjoy the blessings of those sulphur springs to which nobody has paid the slightest attention.

"My motto is simple: it is better to have imagination than a good education. I didn't go to school, I couldn't go to school, but I don't regret it. I began my career with a machine gun in my hand, fighting reactionaries, and people imagine that I must still defend myself with the machine gun, not knowing that it is a flower that really protects me."

He had picked a spray of budding flowers and was holding it delicately in his hands. A swarm of butterflies fluttered over the gladiolus, and the thick figure of the boss, his belt loaded with bullets, his pistol, and his avid, penetrating gray eyes, stood out as harshly as that of an outlaw who tries to fool his victims by disguising himself with the symbols of well-bred, fortunate men.

That innocent spray could not disguise the silent, eloquent brutality of his pistol, nor those fields where the butterflies flew, the truth hidden under their flowery mantle. Some of his lands, as a matter of fact, he had bought at the beginning of his career, using force, bribery, or armed persuasion, but since he could not buy the fields at Santiaguito adjoining the highway planted in gladiolus, because they were communal lands, he rented them from the Indians for a pittance.

No one could say how much land Don Ulises possessed, or what tactics he had used in order to acquire it, since everything that was known of this contradictory man was known indirectly, owing to certain indiscretions or certain strange, doubtful, or scandalously melodramatic events. From time to time rumors spread concerning owners of land who refused to sell it and were beaten up, nor was it rare either that a drunken Indian would refer bitterly to his status as an ill-paid laborer, while Don Ulises enriched himself by cultivating *his* lands, and occasionally people came to be aware of an abuse only because the victim disappeared, or because the boss's gunmen, in their daily parade, had indeed to emphasize their arrogant insolence through an excess of professional pride.

I am not fixing facts in my memory. Rather, I am recording rumors, obscure and not very consistent events that give an idea of the climate of terror in which we lived. There was as much distance between the pretended revolutionary-civilizer-father of a family, generous host-protector of the Indians, and the rapacious-luxurious-petty-tyrant-exploiter, as the metaphysical distance that existed between his machine gun and the spray of white flowers he held devoutly, delicately, like a scepter of patriarchal rule and everlasting idyll.

23

Doña Paula had not lost her status as legitimate wife. She was the heart of the official, respectable house, and upon her fell the responsibility of a complicated administration. The big house on the highway sheltered her only son, young Ulises, already married, her grandchildren, a divorced daughter named María, and frequently a multitude of poor relatives who sought the shadow and protection of the boss. In the rear of this enormous mansion were the sawmill with its office force and laborers, Don Ulises's offices, wine cellars, storerooms and silos, rooms for the guards and gunmen, many of whom ate at the house, and if that were not enough, the boss, following the custom of the landowners, gave lodging to and dinners and parties for numerous guests, all of whom were people of importance, industrialists whom he might possibly make partners in his businesses, prominent politicians and journalists who would mention him and defend him from the attacks of his enemies.

Just by reading the newspapers, I could form an idea of the progress of his affairs, his needs and his projects, because while Don Ulises enjoyed being generous and was fond of conversation and giving receptions, he never lost sight of the practical advantages he could obtain from a well-managed hospitality.

He organized the details of his parties with a meticulousness bordering on pedantry and, in general, conferred on the minor acts of his life an importance and significance of their own in which the stamp of his unmistakable personality could easily be observed.

Don Ulises was convinced that a man of standing must

surround himself not only with an apparatus capable of emphasizing his importance, but with a certain reserve, with a system of security which would permit him to handle his business without indiscreet witnesses or spies in the pay of his enemies. In order to avoid his servants' being present in the dining room, he had installed a little railroad, mounted on ebony rails and driven by a pulley, that brought the dishes from the kitchen. The toy in question would cross the dining room carrying the soup tureen, Don Ulises would take it, serving himself first—as he said, it was the sacred privilege of the host—and then place it in the moving center of the round table. This center which revolved slowly within the center of the table, propelled by an invisible electric motor, put the platters within reach of the guests and with them the oil, salt and pepper, cheeses, gravy boats, mustard, wine, and liqueurs with which that moving center was generously supplied.

The guests could not disguise their astonishment.

"Tell us, Don Ulises, how did it occur to you to invent this table service?"

"That's an old story. Ten or fifteen years ago, a spy from my enemies heard us talking about a certain political maneuver, and the result was that the maneuver was ruined and two men were murdered in an ambush . . . Then," he added in his hoarse, agreeable voice, "I realized I was living in an enemy world where the slightest indiscretion could cost a man his life. Politics is a complicated game. Crimes are tolerated, but errors—not by any means!"

When Don Ulises, in a burst of speech, thought he might be revealing the *modus operandi* of his politics, he would exclaim, filling his guest's glass:

"Drink up, have some more wine. It's the only foreign thing on my table. The flowers, the suckling pig, the turkeys, the vegetables, the cheese, the fruits are all our own products."

The center of the table turned slowly and unceasingly,

taking the place of servants, and in the doorways, immobile
as statues, the gunmen mounted guard, armed with small
machine guns. In that setting designed to overwhelm his
guests by the display of his feudal magnificence, Don Ulises
felt happy, and as the plates filed past and the wine flowed,
his eloquence became inexhaustible. He knew how to con-
verse with his guests and his trusted men of the things that
interested him, and he possessed a repertory of anecdotes and
stories developed during almost half a century of adventures
and unusual experiences, so that he would resort to it, as to
a fabulous treasure, with the certainty that the brilliance of
those jewels, ancient or modern, evoking violence or idyllic
labors, was going to shine upon his sedentary guests or even
upon his comrades of past forays.

"Did the Indians impress you?" he asked a journalist, low-
ering his head like a bull preparing to charge. "I'm not surprised at anything. From a distance their huts scattered on the
mountain slopes produce a very favorable effect. A European
writer traveled with me over the Indian territory, which we
visited in the morning, and he stopped his horse. 'It's a
little Switzerland,' he commented. 'The pine woods, the
smoke escaping from the huts, the cattle in the meadow, and
the mountain boulders . . .' Yes, a picture-postcard land-
scape. But you have to go up closer. They have no furniture,
no lights, no windows, no food, and the people go about in
rags.

"All my efforts to understand them and civilize them have
turned out to be useless. I see them, touch them, hear them
speak, and I wonder: 'What is there behind those eyes? What
are their true feelings? What are they thinking about?'

"When I was still a young man, I went to one of the most
out-of-the-way little villages in the sierra. The chief of the
tribe, an old man now, had been seriously wounded in one leg
and was lying on his mat, surrounded by witch doctors who
were putting poultices on him and chanting I don't know
what strange incantations. I drove the medicine men away,

scraped the wound with my knife, disinfected it as best I could—sulfa and penicillin had not been invented—and the man recovered. He took a great liking to me. He wanted me to marry one of his daughters and be his heir, but I made him understand that I was married and that I must return home. On the day of my departure the chief took me by the hand, saying:

" 'Come with me. I want you to meet our gods.'

"He led me to a cave, not very far from the town. It was a lofty cave, like a cathedral. It received light through a few crevices hidden among the tree branches, a green light that fell onto the stalactites and boulders, giving them a mysterious air. At the back of the cave there were raised stone altars on which rested two enormous idols garlanded with flowers and offerings and surrounded by a number of little idols. Some kneeling worshippers were drinking aguardiente and reciting their sins in a sharp, lamenting voice.

"The years went by, and I forgot about the cave, the idols, the Indians' song. Who looks back? Who takes pleasure in recollections and turns them over and over, if not the dead? The secret of my vitality consists in not looking back on the past, in my living absorbed in the present with the fixed idea of carrying out the frequently very heavy duties which destiny has seen fit to pile on my shoulders. I've been watching you," he said, interrupting himself, "I've been watching you, and I see you are slighting my wine. Three times this bottle of Pommard has passed in front of you, and you've made no effort to take it."

"Your stories are to blame for distracting me," the journalist said.

"Do they really interest you?"

"More than you imagine. Go on now with your story of the idols."

"It had an unexpected ending. Two or three weeks ago some archaeologists from the capital, accompanied by soldiers—I suspect a priest in the area had revealed the existence of the cave—arrived in town, and notwithstanding the entreaties of the Indians, or their tears, *or* their rights, they carried the idols off to Mexico City. The affair is more complicated than it seems. The authorities say that those beautiful pieces—though I don't see any beauty in them anywhere —legally belong to the nation, and the Indians claim that those idols are not idols or archaeological relics at all, but simply their gods, their only, true gods."

"The Indians are entirely right," asserted the journalist. "They should return their idols to them."

"That's my opinion, too, except that the archaeologists don't understand certain things. Really, we know nothing about the Indians. We know nothing about our country. Wherever we reach out our hand, we touch a sacred place. I don't know how to say it to you, but it is as if we were touching a wound. The fields are teeming with gods and ghosts. There are subterranean gods and gods of the air, gods of the mountain, of the waters, of the caverns. The Indians almost never dare to go out at night, but if they do for some reason, they go together, smoking and talking in a loud voice to fend off the evil spirits. I stumbled upon them one certain night, on a path in the woods. No one dared to say a word, because if they open their mouth, their soul will escape, and the spirits that are constantly spying from the mountain will take possession of them.

"Can you imagine a world peopled by malignant spirits whose only occupation consists of robbing the Indians of their souls? A world of witch doctors, of incantations, of strange ceremonies, of magic drugs that enable the initiated to feel themselves gods, to descend into hell and talk with the dead? I have seen them come out of their hallucinations, and I confess to you that I was afraid. They know something that we don't know, and in that secret is rooted their strength to bear their greatest adversities stoically. They could let their hearts to be torn out without stopping their laughter."

Don Ulises was never weary of telling stories. He exercised

upon his guests a kind of hypnotism similar to that of the constant revolution of the table. Generally his parties ended very late, and the boss himself, followed by his gunmen, would go out into the street to say goodbye to his guests. The luxurious automobiles drove off, but still he remained a while in the open air, savoring his triumph.

These important people were not visiting the unknown, unimportant town of Tajimaroa, but were visiting *his* house. They came attracted by his fame and the magnificence of his receptions, but somehow something of that social prestige fell upon our village and increased the stature—already large in itself—of Don Ulises Roca.

While his wife had to put away the silver, remove the tablecloths, and straighten up the house, Don Ulises would go off to Santiaguito, from which he returned punctually at eight o'clock in the morning in order to undertake, officially, his daily visit to the Ayuntamiento.

At nine, after a plentiful breakfast at which his family was present, he would install himself in his office at the sawmill which he operated behind the house and dedicate himself to public or private affairs. His anteroom was the anteroom of a governor's office. Problems of the unions or the peasant groups, land matters, bribes, swindles, and the subtle or crude maneuvers which our small-town politics demands, as well as various transactions, gifts, and employees' petitions and favors were aired in that office which I visited one day, trying to seek a reconciliation, as I shall mention later to Your Grace.

At noon, without unduly concerning himself about the people who were waiting for him in the anteroom, Don Ulises would betake himself to his little rose garden located at one end of the house, where he kept his peacocks. I must say I shall never manage to reconcile his passion for machine guns and telescopic rifles with the equally strong passion that Don Ulises felt for those birds, those pictures of serenity, elegance, and vanity. Possession of them was not enough, and he had ordered them reproduced on the great leaded glass of the porch where it went down into the garden, in such a way that the gentle roses and enameled tails of the authentic peacocks could be admired through the rigid tails and false roses on the glass.

As soon as the birds became aware of their master's presence, they would run toward him with their slender necks outstretched, and for the space of a quarter-hour an exchange of well-modulated sounds would take place, a dialogue of soft cacklings, of cluckings, of approvals, and protests, to which the neighbors listened every day (an iron fence separated the garden from the highway), without getting over their astonishment, not because Don Ulises was capable of learning the creatures' language, but rather at his showing a solicitude and a friendly compassion that he never revealed in his dealings with them.

24

Men, like the moon, have two faces. One remains voluntarily removed from view and from the most exacting investigations. The other, the visible one, is of so complex a nature, it encloses so many contradictions under the common irregularities of its face that it is almost impossible even for those of us who have access to the hidden half to penetrate into the meaning of those two faces without running into serious distortions.

Don Ulises's hidden face, the one with his love for Elena, the one with his ambition, and the one with his hate, will always remain in shadow. The one he shows the world is nothing but a tangled sketch, a set of arbitrary lines in which are mixed the pride of the proprietor, the fantasy of the storyteller and of the creator of wealth, the penchant for peacocks and machine guns, and the indifferent cruelty with which he crushed opponents of his schemes.

Nevertheless, those intersecting lines, crude or fine, simple or baroque, do have a contour, do outline a recognizable figure, and this figure can only be that of the boss. With all his contradictions Don Ulises was at bottom the undisputed master over a wide area, the master of the destinies and fortunes of thousands of men, the kingpin in his political games, the strong man of Tajimaroa. All this existed, triumphantly, Monsignor, in spite of the people's increasing hatred; it was an active, living, indestructible reality, a will to dominate like that of the absolute kings; majestically and divinely despotic, it spread itself, outside the law and the conventions.

As a matter of fact, the impression that Don Ulises still left at the end of 1958 was that of a miraculous survival. Time had devoured his wife, the original companions of his armed forays, the first generation of his vassals, and he was living exactly as he had lived in 1930, that is, with his machine gun in hand, his same ambition to command and his same recipes: "My politics," he used to say, "is the politics of simple slogans: money for my friends, a beating for the discontented, bullets for my enemies."

This slogan, which had given him a sinister reputation ever since the beginning of his career, had possibly been softened in the course of the years, and the last part, the one referring to bullets, remained only as a warning, provided that the first two continued in effect, as the case of Manuel and the form in which little neighborhood chiefs prospered could attest.

For the conqueror of time, his origin as a man of the people, his wretched youth no longer counted. He lived proudly in the present, squandering his vitality on the exhausting games of love and politics, without realizing that times had changed and that he was an old man of sixty-three from whom his relations with Elena exacted an effort even beyond his remarkable physical powers, as I could observe on the day he had their first child baptized. Elena was standing beside the baptismal font and excitedly holding in her arms the bundle of red flesh which screamed as it felt the cold water on its little head. His appearance was that of a countryman dressed for Sunday. He wore a new suit, and his badly knotted tie gave him visible annoyance. His gray eyes were fastened on the girl, and in his glance I could read, with downright surprise at Elena's having recovered her graceful, lithe figure, that dark fire—that disturbing fire of sixty-year-olds—which was devouring him.

The wheel had come full circle. A violent desire for love, a timidity in the face of the mystery that the unknown woman has for the mature man, made him abandon his old mate and force the doors of the paradise of which adolescents dream. Doña Paula knew all about it and accepted her fate with resignation, a fate, furthermore, that the majority of the old women and not a few of the young ones in Tajimaroa unfortunately shared, but his deserted wife did not know then that her pain and scorn were being avenged. Time was beginning its retaliation, and Don Ulises was already paying for his triumphs with jealousy, with an increasing and weary impotence—in a word, with that almost perceptible fissure which was threatening to destroy the reasons for his pride.

25

Perhaps Your Grace still remembers the omens that preceded the birth of our volcano. Barnyard fowl and birds stayed awake at night; dogs howled, the ground shook softly, and in the afternoons a reddish fog spread over the narrow valley where Paricutín was to rise a week later, vomiting fire and ashes.

The inhabitants of that ancient volcanic region rocked by earthquakes did not consider the fog of any importance; it did not worry them that the earth was dancing a little more than usual, nor did they think it odd that the telegraph, located thirty kilometers away in Uruapan, functioned only because the local birds were unable to arrange their sleep in a satisfactory manner.

Something similar to all this was taking place in Tajimaroa. Hatred for the boss's rule had been flaring up again, and people were referring to Don Ulises with unusual persistence and irritation. Parishioners would come to the church office and begin telling me their everlasting problems, turning their hats or twisting their shawls in nervous hands, and whether or not it was appropriate, Don Ulises's name would come out.

The merry-go-round set up by the boss—ritual parade, election frauds, daily annoyances—went around continually, and it was useless for the townspeople to try to escape. They retreated twenty or thirty years because the merry-go-round projected its images onto the most hidden folds of their consciences, and that destructive monotony, cruel and inexorable, plunged them into a paroxysm, into a state of constant rage whose danger they did not admit, owing perhaps to the fact that they had been living in irritation and anger since childhood.

"Will you never weary of talking about Don Ulises?" I would say to them.

"It's a sickness, like malaria," they would answer. "We carry it in our blood."

"We can't take any more, señor cura. What does he do with our money? The palace"—they never ceased to apply that name to the shabby Ayuntamiento—"is falling to pieces, the streets—you have seen them—are full of ruts, there are no police, no parks, not even a library where our children can study."

"What about the gunmen? They create rows in the cantinas, they call us cowards, and if we protest, they throw us in jail."

"Yesterday," another complained, "they slapped a fine on me. An unjust fine, believe me, for revenge, just to prevent me from selling a lot to Don Ulises, and this I won't forgive, señor cura . . ."

"Well," I told them, interrupting them, "what do you intend to do?"

"We don't know," they mumbled, upset. "We're a town full of chickens, and Don Ulises's thugs are right about that."

I was passing a store in the plaza, when the fat shopkeeper, his scissors hanging at his waist, came out to me in the doorway.

"Tomorrow is the anniversary, señor cura."

"What anniversary?" I asked, puzzled.

"The anniversary of my son's death. The one Don Ulises's thugs murdered."

I came to think—my state of mind was approaching despair—that the people were talking about the boss, not with the idea of unburdening themselves, but in order to keep the flame of their hatred burning. That series of real or imaginary offenses constituted their daily nourishment. In the market, in the plazas, in the stores, on the sidewalks, when they took their chairs outdoors and organized their conversation groups, they appeared, with their heads bent—they were afraid of informers—to be given over to examining their wrongs in detail, to chewing them untiringly, incessantly, so that our town gave the impression of having been transformed into a gigantic mill of hate, or into a stable where they ruminated an inexhaustible fodder of wrongs and rancors.

As in my days as a vicar, my appeals to resignation, to wisdom, to Christian charity served only to ferment that acid mass further, and I ended—I scornfully remember that new effort now—by inventing my own line for separating religious power and civil power into two clearly defined camps, but this convention too was an inadequate device, since we do not know where one begins and the other ends or how they enter into the life of a town.

The brute force of the boss's rule, the imposition of which was destroying the idea of justice and liberty, the very fact that civil power was the heritage of the bandits and not of the virtuous, was forcing an undermining of moral values against which I could not fight without abandoning my field and turning myself into a rebel.

My fault perhaps consisted in not seeking your advice in time, but what solution could Your Grace have offered me? Wherever there is a rural parish, there is always a boss, and this is the dilemma: either you accept him, or you fight him; either you are a conformist, or you are a true Christian. There were no religious problems in my parish. Children were born and baptized; young people fell in love, and we arranged their weddings; no sick man died without receiving the sacraments. We worked day and night saying masses, teaching the word of God in scattered hamlets, although, Monsignor, people would have preferred a little less devotion and doctrine and a little more justice and liberty. The evil was there, like a tumor that made them spend their lives worried and full of rage, and since religion was incapable of rooting it out, they disregarded that and at bottom began to look distrustfully at me.

I refused to understand that irritation, that deliberate cultivation of hatred, was obscurely favoring their desire for liberty. I did not discover the hidden relation between the two apparently divorced sentiments, but I instinctively felt that we had gone beyond the limits of tolerance and that a great, mysterious danger was threatening us.

26

That was the situation one afternoon in mid-November when a fire broke out on the mountain. At seven o'clock I could see from my cloister the ring of fire advancing on the distant slopes and the cloud of smoke rising to trespass on the starry sky.

An hour later, engineers and foremen from the lumber company went through the town recruiting volunteers to extinguish the fire. Without anyone asking me to, I ordered the alarm sounded, hired several trucks and went off to the mountain in the parish jeep. When I arrived, two kilometers of woods were burning, the adjoining pine groves were quivering with a presentiment of the threat, and the dry pasture, that pasture full of wheat which in summer mixed its sweet aroma with that of mint and thyme, was on fire, crackling and writhing.

The parishioners—at least five hundred of them—were chopping down the pines with their axes or, armed with thick oak branches, were battling the flames without regard for being burned or for the trunks that fell from time to time wrapped in smoke and whirlwinds of sparks.

By midnight they had managed to control the fire. The men had a strange appearance. Their teeth shone in their black faces wet with perspiration, and in spite of weariness and their poor clothes (perhaps their only clothes) being torn, they were singing happily.

A week later *El Diario* in Morelia published an unexpected news item: the lumber company, desirous of showing its gratitude to the "volunteer saviors of our forest wealth"— as the notice said—had decided to recompense them by depositing the sum of twenty thousand pesos with the town council so that "this respectable body" would be responsible for its distribution.

Thinking they had the money in their pockets, the surprised townspeople—they had worked disinterestedly without expecting any reward—appointed a committee charged with collecting it, but the days went by, the committee wasted its time and cooled its heels, and the mayor kept the money, producing trifling excuses which only increased peoples' irritation.

On the tenth of December, almost a month after the fire was extinguished, it was officially announced that the twenty thousand pesos had been set aside to pay the old debt contracted by the town council for repairs to the drinking fountain, and this new fraud—the waterworks in question had been paid off by means of special contributions without a bill ever being presented to the citizenry—was added to the chain of past frauds, and the tension became unbearable.

The boss was talked about openly, the people, who were ready to have it "all come out at once," disregarding the consequences, and as they feared, Don Ulises responded by jailing and beating the rebels, for he was of no mind to allow disrespect, or a "town full of chickens"—those were his very words—to trample the principle of authority underfoot.

There began a period of revenge and repression without a foreseeable end, and I thought that my duty lay in speaking to Don Ulises. Perhaps I had no other way out. I recovered my hope of being listened to, of attempting a reconciliation, and one morning, not without doing violence to myself, I presented myself in his office at the sawmill.

27

He was sitting at his desk next to a window, bathed in the strong yellow midday light. His vigorous figure seemed to be made of a roughly pruned, solid block of wood. His short red neck supported a round head with grayish hair; his little eyes looked out harshly under his thick brows; his chest lifted his wool shirt and appeared broader than it really was because of the disproportion existing between the breadth of his Herculean torso and the smallness of his legs, which were bowed from his habit of riding horseback.

In spite of his sixty-three years, the well-shaven skin of his face did not show too many wrinkles. He moved heavily and surely, like a chief accustomed to command and be obeyed without question, and he spoke rapidly, without a coastal accent—he had been born in Veracruz—in a harsh, yet agreeable voice that softened the hardness in his eyes.

Seeing me in the doorway, he got up and offered me a seat. "Sit down, señor cura, and tell me how I can serve you."

"I need wood for the school roof at San Bartolo, Don Ulises, and I thought you might make me a present of it."

"Consider it done. One of my trucks will take it to San Bartolo tomorrow."

On his desk rested a machine gun, two or three loaders, an oil can, and cotton waste—when I entered, he had been busy cleaning it—and on the wall were hung guns and hunting rifles.

"You caught me red-handed!" he exclaimed. "You'll be thinking the chief is getting ready for a new foray, won't you?"

"Why do you want weapons, Don Ulises?"

"I couldn't live without them. They're my hobby, as the Americans say."

"It's a deadly hobby, Don Ulises."

"That's as may be. Many years ago—why not admit it?—poverty obliged me to leave Veracruz and seek my fortune elsewhere."

He went to the window and looked for a long time at the countryside.

"I came through here, and I liked those woods, those green pine woods, those clearings where the herds are pastured. Are you from Zinapécuaro?" he asked, turning toward me.

"I am from Zinapécuaro, and I understand your fascination with these mountains very well."

" 'Fascination'?" he asked himself. "That is exactly the word I was looking for. The woodlands fascinated me. I bought a secondhand axe and became a woodcutter. Look at my arms, señor cura"—he rolled up his shirt-sleeves, showing me his muscular arms patterned with prominent veins— "with these arms I chopped down thousands of pine trees. I worked like a madman, and do you know for whom I worked? For men who had machine guns and bodyguards and bought woodlands from the Indians for a pittance and paid their woodcutters starvation wages. I soon learned my lesson, señor cura. I bought a machine gun, rebelled against the scoundrels, and then they respected me. In Mexico they despise a man without a pistol," he concluded thoughtfully, while he held out his freckled hands (on the left bulked the stump of his index finger, mutilated in his days as a woodcutter) as if he were seeking the protection of his machine gun.

"Those were different days, Don Ulises, and forgive me for speaking to you with the same frankness. Nobody today stands for being subdued by force, much less by armed force."

He stopped laughing, and his face hardened.

"Explain yourself clearly, señor cura. I don't know whether that is an innuendo or a sermon."

"Sermons aren't of any use with you, or innuendoes either. It's a warning. The people are beginning to tire of you and your thugs."

"What 'thugs'?"

"The municipal president, the secretary, the commandant of police, the councilmen . . ."

"You appear to be suffering from some confusion. The municipal authorities are one thing, and what you call my 'thugs' are another."

"Let us forget this playing with needless ironies, Don Ulises. As the priest of Tajimaroa I have come to tell you that the people hate you, and that this hate can turn out to be dangerous for you."

"Why do they hate me? I'm respectful to all of them."

"They hate you because you have dominated the authorities for thirty years."

"Señor cura," he exploded, pounding his desk, "don't stick your nose into politics, as I don't stick mine into your parish affairs! Those spiteful people have got you all excited."

"Politics is not my affair. I only came to warn you of the existence of a real danger, of an increasing discontent which must not be disregarded."

His anger disappeared, and he adopted a conciliatory tone.

"Tell me, señor cura, without beating about the bush, what do the people want?"

"They want liberty . . . That is, something they have never had."

"Now, that's the word I was waiting for all the time. 'Liberty!' No, señor cura, pardon me for saying it, but you don't know your parishioners. They are too stupid, too subservient, to understand what liberty means and to take advantage of it. We Mexicans are afraid of liberty."

He spoke firmly and gave the impression that the subject was familiar to him. His words filled me with astonishment. That man leaning on his machine gun was speaking like the Grand Inquisitor in Seville, perhaps without having read Dimitri Karamazov's poem.

"What would your flock do if I were to leave Tajimaroa, if they were free to choose their own authorities?" he asked, becoming more excited as he spoke. "They would choose the worst exploiter, the most ambitious, most reactionary man, and they would end up wishing for my return and attributing to me qualities that I don't have. Do you doubt that? I will give you an example. We had a despot, a tyrant who ruled the country with an iron hand for thirty years: his name was Porfirio Díaz. Under his dictatorship there was no freedom of the press, no political liberty, no personal liberty. The campesinos were slaves of the feudal lords; the army repressed the strikes of hungry workers with bullets. The journalists who fought against his dictatorship went to jail. One day a rich little man arrived, an idealistic man, mentioned the word 'liberty,' that word you like so well, and just by mentioning it he overthrew the tyrant. Months later that little man who gave Mexico its longed-for liberty began to be hated and ridiculed. Without the hindrance of a gag and without the danger of dying murdered in jail, the journalists mocked him, heaped ridicule upon him; ambitious men, already stripped of their chains, organized rebellions in order to gain control; peasants and workers rose against their liberator because they wanted bread and not liberty, and the little man wound up murdered. Two, three, five years after his death people did not remember their liberator, their apostle, but they did, on the other hand, feel a nostalgia for their bully, for that old scoundrel who maintained concentration camps and left the enemies of his dictatorship rotting alive. Half a century has passed, and every time the figure of Porfirio Díaz covered with debris is thrown onto the screen, people shiver with pride and applaud enthusiastically, because they don't want liberty, but authority, they don't want democracy, but strong men to obey and revere as they have done since the days of Emperor Moctezuma. Among us liberty is a dream, or it is a nightmare, but never a reality."

"You are mistaken, Don Ulises. Mexico is no exception. Like all countries she has fought heroically for liberty, except that she has never been able to achieve it. In the hour of triumph her liberators have been transformed into her new oppressors and have defrauded her, so that ours is a people who have not enjoyed a single hour of liberty, who have been sacrificed for it and have seen it vanish, have been robbed of it in one form or another, which has only increased their desire and hunger to possess it. Other civilized peoples have shown themselves as eager to give up their liberty as their fathers were to fight for it, but this is not our case. Deprived of what is considered a supreme good, in the eyes of those who suffer oppression and despotism liberty still keeps all her prestige intact, all her magic and all her hope."

"Authority needs force in order to exist and consolidate itself, and we are all of us fooling the people. You yourself, señor cura, are my accomplice in spite of yourself. You live by false miracles, by mystery, and you promote superstitions in order to keep the people deceived. Perhaps you did not accept the prophecy of darkness? Has not your role perhaps, the role of the Mexican church, consisted of allying yourself with the powerful and of preaching resignation to the oppressed, offering them the delights of heavenly paradise in exchange for their earthly wretchedness? Why don't you preach resignation to your parishioners so they can bear my tyranny? Why am I a revolutionary? Of course, we are not perfect, I recognize that, but we *have* given land to the campesinos, and we *have* freed the workers. We keep the peace somewhat by force, because if this force is crushed—bear this in mind!—we would sink into chaos, into the most horrible anarchy."

"I do not deceive anyone, nor do I put a gun to anyone's chest so he will do his Christian duty, Don Ulises. I am a village priest, a priest who was born into and has shared the life of the oppressed. I am against the powerful, whether they call themselves reactionaries or revolutionaries. I believe in the dogmas of my religion, and I try to make less difficult the existence of the poor and of those who suffer injustices and vexations. We are all guilty, and we are all sinners, I humbly recognize that, too. People come to me because they find a consolation in religion, because it signifies a spiritual strength, an escape from the injustice and misery in which they have always lived."

"They used to live worse before, you must admit."

"Half a century has not gone by without some gain. The landlord doesn't exploit the worker ruthlessly now, but the revolutionary leader does exploit him and keep him subdued. The campesino has been freed from his old feudal lord, but he continues to be the slave of his own wretchedness, his isolation, and his ignorance. You, Don Ulises, cannot be ignorant of all that, just as you cannot be ignorant of the real conditions under which the people of Tajimaroa live."

"I gave them water and electricity."

"I am not your enemy, or your accomplice, or your ally. I am the priest of Tajimaroa, a priest who penetrates, very often with repugnance, into the secrets of their hearts, and for this reason I came to tell you: you are running a grave danger, Don Ulises, but there is still time to avoid it. Get rid of your men, give up your machine gun, call for free elections, with the love and respect of the people."

"Thank you for your advice," he answered, forcing a laugh. "You listen to the most reactionary, the most spiteful people, but you do not listen to my peasants or my workers. If I wished, I could have two thousand men here in two hours, armed and ready to defend me. No, señor cura, our methods are different. I do not believe in yours, nor do I try to change them. You do not believe in mine, but you undertake to give me lessons in government."

"I am sorry I disturbed you," I excused myself, considering the interview finished.

"Tell your parishioners that Ulises Roca will not leave Tajimaroa, nor will he dismiss his men or give up his machine gun!" he cried, becoming angry once more. "Tell them I don't care about their hate or their gossiping. They detested me for thirty years, but they came here to sit in this office and beg favors and jobs from me, and to ask me to be their best man or godfather, and to speak evil of each other, and to tell me their stories and their predicaments, and to bow before the boss they call a murderer and a thief."

I hesitated in the doorway.

"Shall we never succeed in understanding each other?"

"It turns out to be difficult. In any case, your kingdom is not of this world. Mine is here, in this town, and I know the way to rule it."

"I have nothing more to add."

"Go with God, señor cura. You'll have your wood at San Bartolo tomorrow without fail."

I did not go again to Don Ulises's house. Shortly after my interview the battle began that was to take away his power, and this coincidence viewed as a proof of complicity decided me to abandon the ranks of the fainthearted and go on to figure in the list of the rebels and the discontented.

28

Meanwhile, vacation time had arrived. The young people who were studying in Morelia and Mexico City had returned home, and the girls were looking forward to their customary two months of promenades and chats at their windows, without the sad farewells and bitter tears that would be shed abundantly at their departure—a fatal ending to every vacation period—being able to cool their initial enthusiasm.

It was soon apparent that the students had changed a great deal that year. Instead of making their rounds calling at the girls' windows or organizing serenades—in winter there was no dearth of music in the streets—they held mysterious meetings behind closed doors.

There was plenty of comment and gossip, as Your Grace may suppose. Some of the townsfolk spoke of obscure anarchist or Bolshevik maneuvers—those were the two terms most often heard. Others swore they were concerned with making infernal machines, and pious versions were not lacking to the effect that the committees were only a pretext to cover up gambling games or, at best, sessions of magic and spiritualism.

The mystery was partly cleared up a week later. The young men rented an old abandoned hall, brought in tables and benches, and fastened a sign over the door saying: Tajimaroa Students' Association. The oddest thing about it was that not just the students came to the association meetings, but workers, businessmen from the plaza, drivers, and artisans, who filled the hall night after night and stayed until early morning, making lofty speeches or discussing political problems with a disconcerting frankness.

Your Grace will ask me what those student meetings consisted of. At the beginning I knew nothing about any of it.

A pharmacist on the plaza made the following unexpected allusion:

"I am frightened and confused, señor cura, in the face of the students' determination. Imagine this—they have proposed to end the boss's rule!"

My feelings were more or less those of the pharmacist. Life had taught me to bear the brutality of the powerful with resignation, and I judged the students' decision dangerous and sterile. "What can they do," I wondered, "against Don Ulises's subtleties and influence? Behind him, as in a Chinese puzzle, is a larger boss, and behind this boss one of still greater stature who manages the police, the army, the judges, and the law." Their audacity was a youthful unburdening, a torpid dream of liberty which would be ridiculously drowned in a pool of blood, as other dreams throughout our history have been drowned.

Fortunately, the young men did not see things with that pessimism. Manuel Espino was at the head of the rebels, and two weeks after organizing the association he sent me a letter, or rather a paper, with two lines that said:

"*Señor cura:* I do not visit you so as not to compromise you. Be calm. Things are going well, and the boss will be overthrown before you imagine. Wait for my news and give me your blessing. *Manuel Espino.*"

Actually, Manuel had kept me informed through various people of everything that happened in the committees, and later, when he won the battle, he gave me a detailed report of what had taken place at the meetings.

(I quote almost word for word a fragment of discussion which will give Your Grace an idea of the spirit that marked these committees.)

Manuel declared:

"We demand freedom to choose our officials."

The workers and campesinos scratched their heads, and their mouths fell open in surprise.

"Yes," they responded, "that's what we've wanted for thirty years, only it isn't easy."

Manuel uttered a peal of laughter.

"Can ten men dominate us? Us? A town of fifteen thousand inhabitants?"

They felt ill at ease under their faded skin jackets. They shuffled their feet and squirmed in their seats.

"What are we to do? What can we do?" they asked.

"First of all, stop being afraid."

A workman got up. His hands grasped the back of the seat in front with such force that the wood creaked. He spoke with his eyes on the floor, with restraint and determination.

"Manuel," he began, "listen to what I'm going to say to you. I'm a workman. I earn twelve pesos a day, and I support my wife and my two children on that money. I'm not afraid of being beaten, I'm not afraid of losing my job, I'm not afraid of Don Ulises, but that is not enough. Courage alone won't get you anywhere. Answer a question from all of us: what do you really intend to do? How will you defeat Don Ulises?"

"You're right," Manuel said, when the workman had finished speaking. "Courage is not enough. In addition to being brave, you have to be organized. You ask what I shall do to overthrow the boss? I'll get people to unite as one man and demand justice."

"I've never seen any justice in Tajimaroa," an elderly merchant called out. "I don't know how you can swallow what you call justice."

"Justice is being governed by decent men; justice is knowing how the people's money is spent; justice is living in peace and without fear. Justice is having a library, a gymnasium, a park for the children, paved streets . . ."

"The streets are filthy," several men said. "We run the risk of breaking a leg at night."

"We need garbage trucks," suggested a market vendor.

"Yes, yes, garbage trucks! Garbage trucks are very important," chorused the enthusiastic followers.

"Everything that we haven't had in thirty-five years, that we could buy with our own money."

From this fragment, Your Grace will judge that the students were not asking for the moon, but for very simple things, things as common as a garbage truck or as indispensable as being free of the humiliations, sneers, and plunderings of the boss's rule. They were asking to breathe a bit of clean air, for more services and fewer pistols, for books instead of drunken brawls, and a gymnasium instead of polished trucks.

29

Don Ulises did not consider the meetings important. In his heart he felt that he was a giant, an exceptional man surrounded by pygmies to whom it was enough to show his machine gun for them to run away in fright. He thought that the youthful rebellion would allow him to open a necessary escape valve—the political pot had been boiling too long—and that in exchange for tolerating a few shouts and listening to some tedious commonplaces regarding democracy and free municipalities, he would be able to make out a list to include the most dangerous of his enemies, without missing a single one.

If the boss had read *Faustus*, he would have exclaimed, rubbing his hands: ". . . I forgive you, good children. Now bear this in mind. The devil is old—therefore grow old in order to understand him."

Except that Don Ulises had grown fat, and his impotence

forbade him to carry out the neat armed strikes which had given him such a reputation at the beginning of his career. While he continued to devote himself to domino games and agreeable visits to his second family, Manuel was winning the favor of the people. He and his companions visited houses, shops, and unions, encouraged the timid, aroused those who were already convinced, captivated the merchants, and the meeting hall proved too small to contain the increasing number of his supporters. The people were becoming aware of their strength. They knew that their enemies had been able to exploit them because they were not united, and this simple truth made them disposed not to desert but to die, if only they could destroy the boss's rule.

I saw the fire grow and did nothing to extinguish it. I went on hiding behind my dividing line, but it would be deceiving Your Grace to say that I witnessed the struggle impartially. I wanted victory for the young men, and not only did I pray for that victory, but I also came to recommend endurance to them and to consider the temptation—it was only a temptation—to join the conspirators.

30

When Don Ulises thought of responding, it was already late. On the same day that he ordered the students jailed, accusing them of being Communists, a rebel column of a thousand men set out for the city of Morelia. I had the opportunity of seeing them. They filed out grouped together in buses, on shabby burros, in private and rented cars, carrying flags and posters. Women came out of their houses to see them off, and the youths shouted:

"Have confidence. We'll soon be free."

One man was weeping on the sidewalk.

"Ay, señor cura," he said to me, "what we old men did not

do in thirty years, the young ones have done in two weeks. It's a miracle from the Virgin."

"Yes," I answered him, "to fight for liberty in Mexico is a miracle."

I am sorry I was not in Morelia that day. To our people were added university students from San Nicolás, some workmen, many curiosity-seekers, and all together, with their flags and slogans, they marched impetuously toward the governor's palace.

The police did not prevent the demonstrators from swarming into the courtyard. Officials came out of their office doors in astonishment, and the soldiers charged with guard duty— a score at most—lined up hesitantly, awaiting orders from their officers.

Ten minutes later a colonel went hastily down the stairs and approached the group of officials who had remained alone in the center of the courtyard.

"The governor," he announced, "is not in Morelia, but the government secretary will talk to a committee of six students."

The secretary received the young men in his office.

"What is the meaning of this disturbance, señores? You did not need to organize a demonstration in order to be heard by the government."

"Señor secretario," Manuel replied, stepping forward, "for years we have sought justice, and the government has never been willing to listen to us."

"Explain your request briefly."

"We ask for freedom to choose our own authorities."

"A legally constituted town council exists in Tajimaroa."

"The town council, señor secretario, has been chosen against the will of the people by our boss, Ulises Roca."

"That fact is not clear to me. In any case, we must wait for the next elections."

"Not at all. We are tired of promises that are never carried

out. Do you know how many years the municipal president
has held office?"

"There are more than a hundred municipalities in this
state, and I don't keep those figures in my head."

"Eight years. The secretary, fifteen. The treasurer, twenty.
The councilmen, four or five, and now we reject them."

"You are allowing yourselves to be carried away by passion.
Instead of shouting and demonstrations, you must draw up
charges. Have you brought a memorandum, a written com-
plaint, a detailed accusation?"

"A memorandum?" Manuel burst out. "We have sent
dozens, and you have filed them away."

"The government does not pick answers out of the air. We
demand proofs, facts that can be verified."

"You demand proofs? The best proof is our city. Go to
Tajimaroa. There is no drainage system, no sidewalks, no
garbage trucks. The streets are dirt or mudholes according to
the weather. The children don't have a park or the students
a library."

"There are dozens of towns like that in Michoacán, in the
whole country, and this situation is not always attributable
to the authorities. Mexico is a very poor nation."

"The money is not lacking, señor secretario, but that
money benefits Ulises Roca's gang, not Tajimaroa."

"You must prove these accusations. The government is
willing to undertake an investigation, and I promise you that
justice will be done. We will get rid of the guilty ones."

"Very well," Manuel said. "When does the investigation
begin?"

"These are things that take time."

"We're tired of waiting, señor secretario. We demand the
removal of the council today, not tomorrow."

"We will not tolerate demands."

"We have tolerated the boss's rule for thirty years. Either
the government throws the council out, or we throw them
out ourselves."

"Is this an ultimatum?"

"Yes, sir, it's a respectful ultimatum."

"You young men are forgetting that the government has the power. Threats do not frighten us."

"On the other hand, you forget what the president of the Republic said. Do you know what he said?"

"Well, he has said so many things . . ." The secretary smiled to hide his confusion.

"It would be a good idea to remember it. 'Bosses last as long as the people want them.' We no longer want the boss, and he will have to leave us in peace. That is final."

31

The government agreed to handle what would afterward be known as the "Tajimaroa case." That same afternoon the chief official left Morelia and arrived during the night, escorted by the people who had attended the demonstration.

The townspeople rushed out into the street carrying torches and waved them, shouting excitedly:

"Long live the students! Death to Ulises Roca!"

They seemed to have come out of purgatory and, of course, Monsignor, I picture that place of torment as a Mexican village where everything is sordid, where repose is colored by alcohol and pornography, and where a boss rules surrounded by bodyguards, by cruel little illiterate, luxurious men, who got rich riding on the backs of a few weary, wretched slaves. Their fatalism, that forced and restless resignation, their resentment toward everything no longer existed now. Humble people left off dissembling and shouted what they had always wanted to shout, without fear of Don Ulises's reprisals.

I remember that night very well. It was carnival time, and a sort of fair had arrived three or four days previously, but nobody wanted to take the children to see the wheel of fortune or to the booths where they display monsters and the well-known pranks of clowns and mountebanks. Members of the company wandered sadly through the streets and were already thinking of leaving to look for a more hospitable town, when the wave of enthusiasm that broke over Taji-maroa caught them up also. They hurried to put on their faded spangled costumes and proclaim the excellence of their performances, leaping about or—since it was a humble fair—imitating the lion's roar. The merry-go-rounds and the shining lighted wheels whirled round, and the gay sound of tin-pan bands and hand organs was mixed with the shouts and exclamations of the crowd.

I have kept my childhood liking for the sword-swallowers who shoot flames six feet long, lighting up the night, for the contortions of the acrobats, and, especially, for those water colors that are hastily done in the little restaurants, and for the booths with toys and masks, bread and colored candy. By the light of torches, oil lamps, and Chinese lanterns, pale faces stand out, consumed by fever and wrapped in shawls, mouths with excellently modeled lips, oblique eyes heavy with threats, sleeping children whose heads hang out and sway dangerously from the rebozos with which their mothers tie them to their backs, and thin, incredibly delicate hands which ceaselessly wave mosquito netting, count copper coins, and offer prayers, dried hares, love letters, songs, little red tarts, tamales, and peanuts for sale.

As in other years, the "spider woman" constituted the fair's attraction. A set of mirrors illuminated by a greenish, opaque light showed the woman's guillotined head surrounded by long legs that moved on a thick curtain. Her black hair, combed in waves and in the little curls of the 1920s, accented the expression of her bland white face, an expression composed of a resignation not lacking in professional pride and the irritation which her eyes with their thick, half-closed lids allowed to show through.

A short distance from the "spider woman," the lighted lobby of the hotel where the chief official was staying seemed to form part of the fair. The man was distinguished from the people who surrounded him not only by his exaggerated elegance—exaggerated, of course, in respect to Tajimaroa— but by the magic powers with which he had been invested. Old women forced their way through in order to touch him with their fingertips, and the townsfolk regarded him anxiously and fearfully, as if he were a magician. At that moment they believed him capable of achieving every kind of miracle. With one gesture he was going to make the boss's rule disappear, and with another release the dove of liberty to fly over the rooftops before the enraptured people, since liberty had in the eyes of my parishioners a concrete, tangible, and beautiful form which might well be that of a dove. They thought that some trivial formalities would be sufficient: they would be given the names of some respectable people, those longest established in Tajimaroa, then the people would assemble and the election of the town council would take place by the classic method of raising their hands.

"No, no, my dear fellow citizens!" exclaimed the chief official compassionately. "I cannot accede to your demands. Tajimaroa is far from being a mere hamlet of a hundred souls."

"What?" cried Manuel, "Is it not enough for the people to gather in the plaza and raise their hands in favor of a dear, respectable neighbor?"

"It is not enough. Unfortunately it is not enough. There is a law which determines very precisely the form in which elections must be carried out. It is necessary for a legally registered political party to exist. Does that party exist?"

"Only the official party exists."

"In that case we must make use of its organization. You yourselves admit it is the only one."

"But, señor," said Manuel, controlling himself, "the official party has imposed Don Ulises's people upon us for twenty years, and no one trusts its proceedings."

"*I* did not invent the voting system in Mexico. People do

vote, of course, but they vote through previously established organizations. The organizations are not improvised, nor are the voters. You must get this through your heads."

Twice during that interminable night I passed in front of the hotel lobby. The chief official's long gesticulating arms suggested the legs of the "spider woman" moving to collect us in her web of lies, and on his bland white face with its half-closed lids was painted her same expression of professional pride and contemptuous irritation.

At four o'clock in the morning, when the fair had ended and the people—residents, clowns, mountebanks—were asleep in their houses and sheds, the chief official, with his stern frown, went up to the rooms that had been prepared for him and slept for some hours.

The hard-fought discussion still went on for two days and nights, and the dilemma was always the same: either they would put up with the boss's rule, or they would elect a new council, using the procedures of the official party.

The students appeared to resign themselves, and the election was carried out in the manner recommended by the chief official. The workers' division of the party (Don Ulises's workers) voted; the peasants' division (Don Ulises's campesinos) voted; the public division (the businessmen, artisans, clerks, farmers, and industrialists who in former years had officially voted for Don Ulises) voted—and the election fell to modest, respectable farmers who were completely indifferent to the public interest.

A great confusion reigned on the morning when the results were made public. Soldiers had arrived from Zitácuaro, and the ancient Ayuntamiento was full of gunmen and armed campesinos whom Don Ulises had brought in from the mountains. On the other hand, it was already known that, the night before, a group of bullies had resorted to the classic procedure of stealing the ballot boxes. They silently broke into the place where these were kept suitably under lock, but at that moment three hundred young men, crouching in the shadows, sprang upon them and, after a brief battle, drove them off with heavy blows.

The chief official did not admit himself vanquished and, fearing the government would lose face, proposed a compromise: the mayor, Guadalupe Cielo, and the treasurer, Luis G. Bolaños, would be eliminated, and the secretary, the councilmen, and the commandant of police would keep their posts, in spite of the adverse vote. The students refused the compromise.

"No," they said, resolutely, "they must all go, down to the last policeman."

The official's embarrassment was visible. He quoted several decrees from the election laws, he spoke of revolutionary unity and patriotism, he held long telephone conversations with Morelia, he threatened to resort to force, and since his reasonings, his threats, and his mastery of the law did not succeed in pacifying the people or resolving the conflict, a deputy—the chief of the official party in Michoacán who, as he said, was skilled in political matters—came to reinforce him. A persuasive, astute man, he objected to the gross, unfair method of the election, he discovered numerous irregularities, and he ended by asking for a census to be taken of the voters, a scrupulous census in which the huts and smallest hamlets of the area would be represented, and that democratic zeal, that show of respect for suffrage in a man who had sanctioned the infliction on them of various bandits without opening his mouth, was too much for the students' patience.

They called the people together, and in half an hour the entire population had gathered in the plaza. It was then five o'clock in the afternoon. At eleven the two officials retired without delivering the desired decision, and the people decided to sleep in the plaza.

The next day, stores and workshops closed their doors, and the market vendors joined the demonstrators. From the church tower the crowd looked like a gigantic multicolored patchwork. They had hung children's diapers in the dry tree branches, and aristocratic ladies protected themselves from the burning sun with sheets and other bedclothes. The people scorned these refinements. Grouped on the walks or on the steps of the monument to Hidalgo, they watched over their children, chatted, or tried to warm a little food. They were all perfectly calm. They seemed to be enjoying the delights of a Sunday in the country, and not even the machine guns pointed at them managed to disturb them.

The soldiers, with their steel helmets, their green uniforms and their clay-colored faces, their slanting eyes, and stiff pursed lips, depersonalized and inhuman, joined together to form a cohesive unit with those soldiers who were watching us slyly from the sidewalks of Zinapécuaro or with those who had expelled us from the seminary.

I could not say if they were the same. The unarmed people —that mass of soft flesh—stood on one side, ready for the sacrifice, and on the other stood that little wall of contention bristling with bayonets, that group excited by a will to destroy so old and repulsive that in order to imagine its equal I would have to go back along the river of time to the cruel looks and stereotyped grimaces of the Aztec gods.

At the end of the afternoon the gunmen who had joined the menaced town council and the armed peasants brought in by Don Ulises, leaning over the palace balconies or from the rooftops, shouted abuses or insulted the students with the purpose of provoking a quarrel in which blood would run, though it was not their cries or their gestures that made me fear a catastrophe, but the soldiers' hypnotic glances. Yesterday as today, a gesture, a suspicion, one degree more of fever in their permanent delirium, in their obsession, and in their icy indifference toward death might have impelled them to shoot—that temptation was almost irresistible—into the crowd thronging into the square.

In this way, with machine guns at our breasts, we spent forty-eight mortal hours, and it was only at dusk on the second day that, thank God, the invisible authorities in whose omnipotent hands rests the destiny of our peoples condescended to recognize the right of Tajimaroa to choose its own council, and a wave of joy ran through us once more. Soldiers, campesinos, and gunmen mysteriously disappeared, church bells began to ring, and the shops opened their doors. The students were borne about on shoulders, and they all congratulated and embraced each other until their bones protested.

I was not, therefore, the author of this rebelliousness against the old, rotten rule, although I must confess to Your Grace that I should have liked to be. While they were fighting to establish the kingdom of public morality, this shepherd of souls, this seeker-out of dirty individual sins, was blessing candles, resins, and matches and making the good people believe that darkness would descend upon the world, while other, thicker shadows were flooding their hearts.

32

Manuel's astonishing victory—and I call it astonishing because nothing like it had ever occurred in the history of Tajimaroa—scarcely changed our situation. Don Ulises, though conquered and maimed, continued to be the district strong man. The necessary lessening of his influence and his income, the interruption of his daily trip to the Ayuntamiento, thus breaking a custom consecrated for thirty-five years of rule and, above all, the open wound in his pride, represented humiliations which he could not endure at the risk of feeling dishonored. In him, as I believe he has expressed it, the idea of absolute command proved to be an essential part of his nature, and he was incapable of understanding that Ulises Roca, the master, the born chief, the political administrator, could fall so low as to be turned into a simple citizen, a man subject to the duties, labors, and petty annoyances which make up the normal existence of the governed.

Of course, he considered it fitting to retain his gunmen, and he did not go out into the street without carrying the machine gun ostentatiously in his hand. Daily he visited committees of workers and campesinos whom he continued to keep by force. His bodyguards not only provoked continual squabbles, but spoke of exacting vengeance, and—what was most alarming—he held secret conferences with the bullies and small-time politicians of the area, which kept us in a permanent state of alarm.

The new town council, composed of peaceful townspeople lacking political strength and weapons, did not feel very secure. On the one hand, desirous of keeping the precarious balance of forces, they were obliged to tolerate the gunmen, and on the other, they had to bear criticism and complaints from the young men who had set themselves up, on the edge of the law, as vigilantes and censors of their functioning. All this silent battle bristling with a thousand disagreeable incidents amounted basically to the fact that Don Ulises did not relax his intention of regaining his lost control, and the young men were not disposed to allow their recently won liberty to be snatched from them.

33

Holy Week imposed a truce. Who was thinking about the boss's maneuvers, about wrongs, and past battles? The drama of Our Redeemer had succeeded in calming their passions, and friends and enemies mingled in the cloth-draped churches, apparently reconciled.

While the beginning of Easter had made me hope for some more tranquil days than those we had lived through during

Lent, on the very night of Resurrection an event of a sportive nature took place, insignificant in itself, which was to be, owing to a chain of strange circumstances, the beginning of the tragic events which prompt this report.

Since morning Avelino had been making the rounds of the taverns in a state of complete drunkenness, uttering threats. He spoke of a blow prepared against the mayor, and many people heard him swear that "on Easter Monday Don Ulises's enemies would bite the dust." The defeat suffered by his chief, a defeat which had cost him personally his command of the police, had put him in a dangerous mood. He had provoked frequent quarrel, and had already on two occasions beaten up young men of the association, excesses which the mayor (always timorous) forgave him, and which people bore as one of the unfortunate legacies left from the boss's rule.

At seven o'clock, after unburdening his spite, Avelino went to the barbershop. Our barber Crisóstomo was getting ready to shave, in a somewhat symbolic manner, the sparse hairs of his beard, and he lay stretched out in the chair, his face covered with lather and a linen cloth over his eyes.

"I tell you the boss's patience is exhausted," he told Crisóstomo, "and you'll be a witness to the drubbing we're going to give those association punks."

At the moment he pronounced these compromising words, twenty young men silently entered the barbershop, surrounded his chair, and one of them tweaked his nose with a certain rudeness.

"Well, well, Crisóstomo, what kind of joke is this?"

"It's not a joke, Avelino," said the young man, imitating Crisóstomo's effeminate voice. "I always begin this way when I can no longer resist my desire to cut my customers' throats."

Avelino tried in vain to pull out his pistol. The youths picked him up bodily and, after running with him for two or three blocks, threw him, just as he was, into the fountain in the plaza.

Seeing the gunman thrashing in the fountain, someone commented in a loud voice:

"The water's been poisoned."

This phrase, which illustrated the idea that people had formed of Avelino, was spoken spontaneously and appeared to be quenched then and there without leaving a trace.

Not content with bathing him, the young men shaved him and carried their harassment even further by tying him to a tree and hanging around his neck a cardboard sign on which was painted a skull and the following words: "For a traitor to Tajimaroa."

Since it was Sunday night, respectable families were occupying the benches, and the young people were promenading around the plaza. They were exchanging their usual flatteries, smiles, and secrets among themselves, trained birds were reading lovers their fortune, and the townspeople were eating their doughnuts and peanuts, indifferent to the torture of their bully.

The bath had left him speechless, and the efforts he made to insult people and free himself from the sign board accented the grotesque comedy of his fat cropped head and his eyes which were becoming crossed because of his anger.

The police came along an hour later and took him home. No one was able to calm him. Deaf to the advice of his young mistress (Avelino must under the circumstances be considered her landlord), he changed clothes, took a knife and returned to the taverns, burning with desire for revenge.

Once again in the street, his insults and provocations—he gave the impression of having gone mad—led the police, under the guise of protecting him, to take him this time to jail, without knowing the particularly painful fate that awaited him.

34

A rumor can only be regarded as a work of the devil. It is a mouth that says a few vague, disquieting words, a few obscure, threatening words that another mouth rounds out and loads with meaning and passes to other mouths, to a hundred, to a thousand, to ten thousand mouths, and in the transfer they are embellished, they are distorted, they are burdened with unlikely peculiarities, and the air of the initial words is transformed into wind and the wind in turn into a hurricane that ends by demolishing everything.

The exclamation uttered when Avelino was tossed into the fountain, that exclamation which at the beginning was only the idea of the water morally contaminated by the gunman's carrion-flesh, did not prevent anyone from enjoying the gaiety of Resurrection Sunday, or from having his sleep, but on Easter Monday the forgotten rumor raised its head among the townsfolk.

Pedro Martínez, one of the plaza merchants, told me:

"I don't know who started the rumor. The harness maker at La Sorpresa stopped at my house very early and warned me, quite alarmed: 'Don't let anyone drink the water in your house. It's been poisoned.' "

When I asked the barber Crisóstomo, the best-informed man in Tajimaroa, his opinion as to the origin of the rumor, he confined himself to shaking his head and exclaiming:

"It traveled on the air. It was like a devil, or like an angel."

Not one of my fifteen thousand parishioners, Monsignor, knows exactly how the thing happened. I spent four or five days making visits in the neighborhoods and the marketplace, I spoke to dozens of different people, trying to overcome their fear and distrust, but I could pick up only a few isolated words—always the same—which do not manage to reconstruct the workings of their anger.

"Turn the faucets off tight," was the invariable order. "The boss has poisoned the springs."

They recalled Avelino's threats ("They'll die of poison on Easter Monday"), they spoke of gates opened at the springs, of a nighttime hauling of cyanide and arsenic, and the children, sent home from school by their teachers, seriously claimed to have seen with their own eyes some of their classmates topple over poisoned in the classroom, kicking and spitting foam from their mouths.

The importance of the rumor was equal only to its absolute ambiguity. To these people, Monsignor, water is precious. Only two years ago they still had to go to the public fountain for it, the same as I did in Zinapécuaro. They keep it, with the utmost care, in the coolest places in their houses, and when they drink, they close their eyes, throw back their heads, and savor it drop by drop, because they relate the pleasure of satisfying their thirst to the pain in their shoulder left by the pole on which they carry it from the fountain. From their grandparents, from their parents comes their zeal to keep it free from impurities, their strong desire not to waste a treasure accumulated at the cost of work and privations, so that the rumor wounded one of their vital centers, perhaps the most sensitive, and the mere suspicion that the water, their water, might be poisoned took away their judgment and plunged them into a frenzied dementia.

At seven-thirty on the morning when the rumor reached the marketplace, the avalanche was rolling, and no one could stop it. They believed in the poisoned water as they believe in holy water, and they accepted its new nature without question, without hesitation. Butchers, sellers of heads and barbecues, tackle dealers, tanners, shoemakers, maté sellers, shawl vendors, and grocers left their steaming pots or their dried birds and talked about dying students, rat poisons, pigs and dogs that were dying disemboweled; the rumors entered the shops and artisans' workshops, and people crossed themselves, exclaiming:

"The water has been poisoned! It's the boss's revenge!"

We were at the end of the dry season. For six months the sky had remained blue, and in the woods frequent fires were breaking out. Not a trickle of water flowed through the rocky bed of the arroyos, and in recent days we had been breathing an atmosphere of dust and smoke that irritated our nerves.

In spite of the early hour, the day began exceptionally sultry. Little clouds like dirty sheep's wool covered the sky, and a thick haze hid the woods and stretched a shimmering veil on the horizon.

Sensing a danger that was not clearly defined, people began to close their doors and head toward the Ayuntamiento, not knowing exactly what to do. It was eight o'clock in the morning.

35

The mayor arrived at the run-down palace at eight-thirty. He had spent the weekend at his bird farm located on the outskirts of town, and less than half an hour ago a brother of his had informed him of the mishap suffered by Avelino on Sunday.

The two hundred townspeople gathered in front of the palace pursued him with questions.

"Keep calm," the mayor advised. "How can you believe such a story? There is no poison that can contaminate so large a volume of water."

"The water is poisoned, señor presidente. We know it for certain."

"What proof have you? Do you know of some poison?"

"They tell us . . . They talk, and when the river makes a noise, señor presidente . . ."

"Go back to your homes, to your businesses. I promise you I'll start an investigation into the springs this very day. We will have the water analyzed."

Not the rumor, but the annoyance to which Avelino had been subjected was worrying the mayor. It was certainly more than Don Ulises would be able to endure. One of his men had been exposed to public derision in front of the mocking complacency of the police, and if he did not proceed energetically, he would be without arguments to defend himself from the charge of complicity which the authorities in Morelia would undoubtedly bring against him.

Resolved to gain an advantage with the boss, he ordered them to bring Manuel Espino to him and, while he waited, he asked for a meeting with the governor of the state.

"The governor," replied the telephone operator at nine-thirty, "is not in Morelia."

"Then put me in touch with the government secretary," the mayor requested.

A quarter of an hour later the operator advised:

"The secretary is at a meeting and will be unable to speak to you until noon."

At ten o'clock Manuel Espino, followed by twenty youths from the association and guarded by the commandant of police, crossed the packed plaza. The atmosphere was suffocating. The artificial stone of the monument to Hidalgo—the hero's delicate bald head seemed like a large egg and inspired a disproportionate melancholy—reflected the sun, and the few trees, stripped of leaves, cast no shade. Having exhausted the bottled soft drinks and the beer without succeeding in relieving the thirst that was tormenting them, the people became increasingly irritable. Seeing Manuel, they began to shout:

"Where are you going, Manuel? Are they taking you prisoner?"

"The president sent for me. That affair of Avelino bothers him."

"We're ready to defend you."

"I ask you just to keep calm. Don't do anything that can compromise you."

As the mayor himself told me afterward, Manuel and several students from the association, possibly under the influence of previous events, had an "odd" appearance that morning. Their eyes reflected a feeling of solitude and sadness that contrasted with their passionate energy. "He seemed to be not of this world," declared a friend who knew him well. "He was with us, attacking and defending himself magnificently, but nevertheless he felt himself to be absent, as though he stood outside that tremendous confusion."

"I had you brought here," the mayor said, "so that you may tell me why you gave Avelino a bath."

"Because you are not punishing Don Ulises's thugs."

"That is my business, not yours."

"We are charged with seeing that the authorities do their duty."

The mayor grew red with anger.

"Might I know who entrusted you with that mission?"

"The people, and if you doubt it, you have only to go out and ask them."

"Well, men, I did not call you here to argue, but to tell you that you have committed a crime and are going to be taken into custody."

"We don't mind going to jail. Maybe that's the place where the best Mexicans are today."

"Manuel, I do appreciate you. I know you are fighting for liberty, that is, for something our people absolutely lack, but you must be reasonable. Liberty is not won by giving rascals a bath."

"Justice is denied us, and we have to make our own."

"I am not denying it to you."

"Nor do you respect it. Don Ulises has meetings every day with his bodyguards; Don Ulises provokes us; Don Ulises is getting ready for one of his strikes, and what are you doing? His bodyguards provoke us; they get drunk, they insult peaceable people, and you give them back their weapons, you let them go free, but us you put in jail. Is that your justice?"

"Don't judge by appearances."

"Your credulity will be the ruin of you. Ulises Roca is capable of any infamy."

The discussion was abruptly cut short. A councilman appeared excitedly in the doorway.

"Come out here, señor," he told the mayor. "They're bringing a poisoned boy."

The crowd had surged into the plaza, the entrance and courtyard of the Ayuntamiento, and they made way, as the waters of the Red Sea must have parted, for the stretcher which six men were carrying on their heads. They managed to make out the boy's livid face and his bare feet covered with clay.

"Do you see?" Manuel asked. "I told you so before. Ulises Roca is capable of any infamy."

36

I know very well what Your Grace is going to ask me, and I hasten to answer you: Don Ulises did not poison the water. If the chemical analyses and the detailed investigations carried out in the springs were not enough to show that there was no such poisoning, Don Ulises's character must be taken into account. He had been capable of dominating his enemies by using violence, except that these exploits proper to an already outdated political style had taken place a quarter of a century ago, and in any case, Don Ulises must be regarded as a petty criminal, as a delinquent lacking imagination, as a man who is mediocre in good and evil to whom his mediocrity prohibited the grandeur necessary to order a mass condemnation of fifteen thousand human beings.

Nevertheless, that boy does exist, that unknown factor which converts the problem of the poisoned water into an undecipherable mystery. "Come," I tell myself, "let us have patience and try to reconstruct the devilish machinery of anger piece by piece." First of all, who was that young fellow? That young fellow, Monsignor, was named Pilar Plata, and he was an illiterate nineteen-year-old peasant who lived with his aunt outside Tajimaroa, in a house next to "Spring Farm," where he worked as a laborer.

On Easter Monday he got up as usual at seven o'clock and had a breakfast of two small slices of melon, some bread and a cup of chocolate. After breakfast Pilar took leave of his aunt, an elderly half-deaf woman overly fond of saying her prayers, went to the farm, and began his daily labor. Within ten minutes he was thirsty, put down his hoe, and from the spring— right there gushes one of the springs that supply Tajimaroa— he drank one swallow, just what he could hold in the hollow of his hands, and went back to work.

In less than a quarter of an hour he felt seriously ill. His cheeks, his forehead, his lips were numb. He tried unsuccessfully to walk; his rigid legs would not obey him. Nor could he move his fingers, and an enormous weariness came over him, obliging him to sit down on the ground.

"Ventura," he managed to say to an old laborer who was working nearby, before he lost consciousness, "Ventura, I'm dying."

Frightened, the old man took him by the armpits and dragged him to the highway, where a truck picked him up, still in a faint, to take him to the Ayuntamiento, where the Red Cross was set up.

These facts, Monsignor, the state prosecutor established after undertaking numerous questionings and several investigations, since in his zeal—very legitimate, certainly—to prove the criminal nature of the rumor, that young man was the key to his entire case. I questioned Pilar too, his old aunt and his neighbors, and I came to the same conclusion as the energetic, conscientious official. Of course, the house is located on the outskirts of town, in a remote district which at nine o'clock in the morning had not yet been touched by the rumor. The neighbors, almost all campesinos, orbit in the space bounded by their houses and the farm fields, and beyond those limits extends, for them, a hostile, unknown world where they seldom go. The young man belonged to that world. With the same obstinate purpose with which men get drunk, lie, or beat their wives, he believed in a God endowed with a beautiful white beard, sitting permanently on a cloud, and in legions of devils who now and then left their subterranean homes. He did not know the meaning of the word "democracy," never felt the necessity of learning to read, and to give an idea of the extent of his innocence, I must say that he had not the faintest idea that a man named Ulises Roca existed.

I might think of a fiendish coincidence, of the spark which the poisoning of that innocent man proved to be falling on the explosive materials accumulated during the years of the boss's rule, but here is where the devil is introduced again, and again I lose the thread of my prosaic deductions. Pilar Plata was not the only one poisoned. Fifteen minutes later a pregnant woman of thirty-five made her appearance, whom her family carried in their arms, and she presented the same symptoms as the peasant boy—a typical picture of poisoning, as the doctors diagnosed it—that bore no relation to her condition, or to the imaginary poisoning of other women treated later at the Red Cross whom the psychosis created by the rumor had made feel ill.

So then, Monsignor, it proves useless to speak of the guilty or innocent, and it only remains for us to resign ourselves in the face of calamitous events. I do not blame Don Ulises, and I strongly reject the implication of an old school text in which Nero appears reclining on his marble couch, contemplating the burning of Rome through a carved emerald. The boss never liked this kind of killing, and therefore our drama lacks expressive images. It is simply a torrent, a freshet, an inundation of waters darkened by the metallic, rusty color of wrath. Only the spirit of the Lord would succeed in stemming that torrent, but the Lord remained mute, devoted to carrying out his work of purity. He had cast up that boy as evidence that the people were demanding to exercise their justice, and that was only the beginning of His terrible vengeance.

37

The chief doctor at the health service was alarmed, as he told me on my return from Morelia. Pilar Plata, stretched out on a bed, was receiving his injection of serum, and the woman, very pale from having vomited, was slowly recovering in the little Red Cross emergency room set up in the basement of the palace.

"I believe," he said to one of his medical aides, "it must be our duty to warn people. They must refrain from drinking water until we know exactly whether it really is poisoned."

One of the young men from the association who was at the Red Cross—the whole town wanted to look at the sick people—heard the doctor's words and stepped forward.

"Doctor, I can easily get a sound truck and warn people, if you like."

"Yes, you do that," the doctor replied, "if only to satisfy our consciences."

At eleven o'clock the vehicle's horns—it belonged to a state secretary—spread the warning through the streets of the town:

"Do not drink the water! You run the risk of death! It's been poisoned!"

In this manner the rumor took on an official character, in fact, which did not admit of any doubt, and the warning voice, penetrating into houses still untouched, ended by sowing disorder and anger.

The boss's intimates declared that the young men who undertook to broadcast the rumor were accusing Don Ulises of having poisoned the water. This criminal inciting has not been proved, and people had already associated the boss in some fashion with the poison, they really believed him capable of committing this crime and, obeying an instinct, they left the palace and began to proceed toward Don Ulises's house.

The house showed no sign of life. The peacocks displayed their enameled tails in the rose garden. The doors and windows facing the highway remained closed, and the entrance giving access to the sawmill, located in the part of the alley which bounds one side of the extensive property, was deserted.

It was eleven-thirty. The crowd, continually swelling, standing in the fiery sun, was dying of thirst, and their rage, so far repressed, found an opportunity of relieving itself. The occasion, anxiously feared and hoped for—of confronting the boss, of forcing him to leave Tajimaroa, of showing him that the people repudiated him—had arrived, and some daring souls, the most excited ones, threw stones and shouted:

"Get out of our city! Out with the boss and his thugs! We want to be free!"

At eleven forty-five came the news of further poisonings (this time actually because of the panic created by the sound truck), and the powerful Red Cross siren let itself be heard like the cry of a mortally wounded animal.

The incessant roar of the siren—that announcement of catastrophe which even in our town has supplanted the church-bell alarm—precipitated the nervous crisis which was already imminent, and stones fell more thickly on the boss's mansion. Then, Monsignor, "that thing" happened. Don Ulises, followed by Adalberto and another bodyguard, came out of the sawmill carrying his machine gun in his hand. He walked slowly along the dusty alley. His presence nullified time, forced it to retreat, to reestablish itself in 1930, when he used to storm city governments and rebellious unions with no other force than his terrible machine gun. "No, it's not a museum piece, a device to make myself respected, the old boss's hobby," he seemed to be telling them while he advanced, threatening and confident.

The people grouped in the alley and on the highway corner stood immobilized. They dropped their stones, and some people began a movement to retreat.

"Cowards, chickens!" Don Ulises shouted in his hoarse voice. "You'll be the ones to leave. Go away right now, or I'll shoot!"

The contempt that his insults revealed—that charge of cowardice repeated through the years—provided an unexpected reaction. Once more the shouting rose, and the stones rained down. The boss stopped, intensely pale. He faced the dilemma of accepting the people's victory and leaving defeated, or of pulling the trigger and shooting into the crowd. His hesitation lasted only a moment. Adalberto, who had kept behind him, fell to the ground bleeding, wounded in the head by a stone, and without thinking further Don Ulises grasped his machine gun and fired.

Manuel Espino was inexplicably struck first. He came running from the palace to join the crowd, and as he crossed the intersection, the burst caught him full force, killing him instantly. Killed there also was an Indian potter from San Bartolo—he had been harnessing his burros loaded with pots and casseroles—and four or five men were wounded and had gone home before the Red Cross appeared.

Men, women, and children fled terrified, and the highway and neighboring streets were emptied in a moment. Don Ulises, propelled by anger, came as far as the corner and went on shouting, beside himself:

"Cowards! A town full of chickens! One man against a thousand, but you flee like rabbits!"

Suddenly he felt silent. He seemed to understand that something irreparable, something that upset the order of things, had occurred, and turning, he went into the sawmill, followed by his gunmen.

38

And I? What was I doing meanwhile? I was making an effort, Monsignor, to read my breviary, pacing the church cloister.

My day had begun very early. At five o'clock I seated myself in the confessional; at seven I said my first mass, the best-attended in a town of devout early-risers, and at nine I had to officiate at a solemn funeral mass. I associate death with violence, and the fact that a young man dies in his bed revolts me like an arbitrary, sly, perverse deed in spite of my familiarity with *in extremis* situations.

The man this morning was not yet thirty years old. He was the treasurer of our savings bank and had died of leukemia in just two or three weeks. Though his lock of brown hair still hung over his yellowish face, his sharp hooked nose, his wasted cheeks, and the bitter despair imprinted on his face had made him unrecognizable. Beside his coffin his mother and his fiancée fought with each other in a resentful contest for the privilege of showing who felt the pain of her loss more, and controlling their nausea, the two endured the strong odor of putrefaction which his body gave off. Outside, the tolling of bells was united with the rumor of the poisoned water like a gloomy foreboding.

I breakfasted indifferently on a little fruit, and at ten-thirty I tried to submerge myself in reading my breviary, without being able to concentrate on it. My wrought-up imagination would not stop recalling the events of Holy Week. I had lived through it intensely, feverishly, minute by minute, and in spite of the fact that Saturday found me worn out, the night, heavy with its announcement of the Resurrection, worked a change in me.

I crossed the church in darkness, wearing my raincape, and as I opened the door, the Easter mystery wafted on the spring night and the presence of the devout who were waiting

eagerly among the shadows of the atrium made me think that
Christ was stirring in His tomb. Shadows covered the world,
and it was I, the unknown old priest, who must put them to
flight, making Him and all those men hidden by the night
return to life.

I rubbed the flint, I drank the holy water, and before I
blessed the fire, the ancient greeting broke from my lips:
"Dominus vobiscum."
In the night a cry rose:
"Et cum spiritu tuo."
Then I traced the cross on the Easter candle—Christ yes-
terday and today—above the letter Alpha, below the letter
Omega—the beginning and end—and I lighted the candle.
"May the light of Christ gloriously revived put to flight the
shadows of heart and mind."

While I was pacing the cloister, I remembered with an
admirable precision my return to the dark church, carrying
the lighted Easter candle, the sudden, profuse illumination
from other candles, the reading from Genesis, the passage of
the Red Sea, Isaiah's prophecies and the song of Moses—
"Await ye my word as the rain"—spoken in the reader's soft
voice, the litany, and at the end the blessing of the water:

"Through God, Who in the beginning with His word
separated you from the dry land, Whose spirit was raised
over you. He Who made you pour forth from the fountain
of Paradise and commanded you to water all the earth in
four streams. He Who, since you were bitter in the desert,
imparting sweetness to you made you drinkable, and drew
you out of the rock for the thirsty people."

My mind, like the hunted stag, rubbed out all the images
of Holy Week and seized upon that innocent, formless crea-
tion that lay in the bottom of the vessel, reflecting the reddish
winking of the candles. As I made the sign of the cross,
scarcely flicking it, the reflected fire blossomed and acquired
the power of blessing, of consecrating and of exorcizing.

Our people alone, Monsignor, are capable of feeling in

their entrails this ceremony, this ritual, in which the spirit
of the Lord descends upon the water and returns it to its
sacred sources, because they are a desert people, a people who
are not migratory but have settled their permanent sights
upon the desert, that ancestral share of black basalt, of
veined granite, of sterile clays or white limestone, where the
leaves of the trees become stunted, where the prickly pear
and agave are covered with parchment and slippery oil, and
where the cactus, protected by thorns and cotton, takes on
the shape of jugs and candelabras in order better to conserve
its water, that precious stream born of the slightest humidity,
distilled through infinite capillary tubes, extracted in miserly
fashion from sand, stone, and hot silica, scratching and dig-
ging the earth as our people scratch and dig it.

To what did they owe that obsession with water? It was
not due to the sultry weather of the dog days, to the greasy,
dusty air they laboriously breathed, but rather to the thirst
and hate in the street, to the warnings of that tragedy being
born outside, and these were beating on my conscience,
making it return again and again to the image of the consecrated water, to the oasis which Resurrection night represented in the midst of our desert.

39

Father Suárez, one of my vicars, appeared in the cloister at
eleven o'clock.

"Things are not going well out there, señor cura," he told
me. "The rumor is circulating that the water has been poisoned."

I closed my breviary and tried to give a sarcastic twist to my
answer.

"How can you believe such nonsense, father? We're dealing with a fraud as old as the world."

"Nonetheless," the father insisted, showing his confusion, "the people are excited."

"It's the heat bringing out these evil thoughts. Don't be alarmed over a trifle."

The father returned half an hour later. His tall, slender figure was waiting at my door, and as I passed him, I suddenly closed my breviary and shot a new arrow at him:

"Part two of the serial *The Poisoned Water*, isn't it?"

"That is so."

"Well, what is going on now?"

"Three people have been poisoned from drinking water, and there is a mutiny in front of the Ayuntamiento."

"What can we do? We are not the health authorities."

"That's true," the father agreed, bowing his head that already showed some gray hairs, and getting ready to return.

"Don't go," I told him, taking him by the arm. "Do you know what I was thinking of when you came with that story? Of the water."

"The poisoned water?"

"No, I was not thinking of that water, but the water we blessed on Saturday, that water returned to its sources which, as it appears, the devil has defiled again."

"I don't believe in the poisoned water, either."

"Let us be calm. Go to the plaza, find out the nature of that rumor, and if we can calm their minds, let me know immediately."

A man appeared at the top of the stairway and exclaimed, choking:

"Señor cura, the shooting has begun!"

"Catch your breath. What shooting are you talking about?"

"Don Ulises has killed two men with his machine gun and wounded three or four."

Not listening to any more, I went into my room, and getting the satchel in which I keep my stole, the holy oil, and a crucifix, I quickly came out.

"Let's go," I told Father Suárez, "and may God bless us."

I crossed the rectory garden, and in two minutes I arrived at the corner where the slain men lay. I recognized Manuel at first glance. His glassy eyes, fully wide-open, were fixed upon a frightful vision. Lifting his beautiful young head, I closed them with the palm of my hand, and his tortured face, that of a furious madman, seemed to depart and to clothe itself again in serenity.

Is Your Grace asking what my feelings were? Manuel was my ideal son, my accomplice in our secret desire to liquidate the boss's rule, the one who, with his purity and valor, carried my dreams of liberty and justice into action, so that for some minutes I was unable to respond, overcome by my rage, my conviction of guilt, and the pain which amputated fatherhood leaves in us.

I had to repress my tears, control the tempest that was unleashed in my heart, and think of the others. Making an effort, I anointed him with the holy oils, commended his soul to the Lord, and ran to the Indian. He was alone—he was simply someone unknown—stretched on the ground, dying. His eyes revealed neither surprise, nor fear, nor despair. They had turned inward and were calmly observing how death approached. The machine-gun burst had cut him almost in half, and he was bleeding a great deal in spurts, soaking the parched earth. I hastened to give him absolution, and a minute later he turned onto his side and died in the same way men die in Zinapécuaro or Pénjamo.

Everything, Monsignor, happened as in a dream. The men, the streets, the trees were real images, they belonged to our world, but they floated deformed in a misty, burning atmosphere, they took on fantastic dimensions, and men and women were filing past with angry faces.

"Go back!" I called to them. "Go home! Don't make the situation any worse."

No one heard me. The whole town was mobilizing to take

revenge, and blood would run in torrents. It was necessary to avoid the drama that was approaching, to try to save the victims and those who would make them victims, and without thinking about it, I set out for Don Ulises's home.

40

I knocked at the entrance in the middle of the alley with both fists. Where the hedges projected, some heads appeared, and from the corners the people assembled in groups shouted to me:

"Come back, señor cura. Come back. Don't deal with the murderers."

Shortly afterward they made way for me, and I went into the sawmill. The machinery had stopped. Don Ulises was at the back of an open passage between piles of recently cut planks. He held his machine gun in his hand, and the handle of a pistol showed at his waist.

"What is this, señor cura?" he asked me. "What do your parishioners want of me?"

"My parishioners, as you will understand, are angry."

"If they attack, I'll defend myself."

"You have killed two men and wounded four or five."

"My machine gun isn't loaded with candy."

His gray hair was disheveled, and his wool shirt rose and fell over his Herculean chest to the beat of his excited breathing.

"Don Ulises, the situation is very serious," I told him, trying not to let myself be carried away by anger. "You must leave town right now. Ten minutes from now will be too late."

"I'll leave Tajimaroa the day this cropped finger begins to grow," he answered, pronouncing his words slowly, while he raised his left hand and held it in front of my eyes. On his hand, reddish and spotted with age, I saw the stump of his index finger. "Do you see that?" he added, with a forced smile. "It still hasn't grown."

The arrival of his wife, his daughter-in-law, and his daughter María prevented me from replying. His wife was wiping away her tears with a handkerchief.

"Dear," she said, choking, "they're burning the house. The windows and the door have begun to burn."

Don Ulises's eyes were bloodshot, and his bull neck grew red. His daughter-in-law, on the other hand, showed not a drop of blood in her beautiful childish face. She was carrying her youngest child wrapped in a shawl, and two other little ones clung to her skirt. His daughter was trembling with rage.

"Order them to give me a pistol, Papá. That rabble has got to learn who we are."

"Don't interfere where you're not wanted. This is a man's affair. Let's go to the house. Come with us, señor cura."

We set out. The house, separated from the sawmill by a hedge, had in fact two floors. The lower, visible only from the interior, was located at the courtyard level; the upper, parallel to the highway, bounded at one end by the house of Don Ulises's only son and on the other by the garden planted in roses which created a corner and led to the street by the sawmill. Don Ulises went up the stairs, still giving instructions to his gunmen.

Through a window of the salon we could see the sidewalk in front and the center strip of the highway invaded by a shouting mob. "Listen to them! They want to kill me, but I won't give them that pleasure," exclaimed Don Ulises, and placing his machine gun on the floor, he drew the blinds and sat down in an armchair.

The light fell sparkling on the peacock tails and roses of the window facing the garden, and I felt as though I were inside those fishbowls where diminutive plastic dragons swim among rocks and artificial coral, not exactly because of the light, but of the house's own atmosphere. Everything in it was conventional and had the stamp of the newly rich; just like the latter's were the rose-colored plaster ceilings, the porcelain toys, the tubular metal armchairs, as were the seascapes or the pianola covered with a velvet scarf on a raised wooden platform.

Don Ulises was carefully inspecting his machine gun.

"There are eight of us men, well armed, who know how to shoot," he said in an undertone.

"Enough of that madness now, Don Ulises. Think of the children, the women of your family."

"They were not willing to leave me in the hour of danger. They are good women and good Mexicans."

His son had entered without my being aware of him. His dark glasses hid his eyes. He was carrying a rifle, and his voice was slightly high-pitched owing to his excitement.

"You, señor cura," he said, pointing his rifle at me, "are responsible for what is happening. You have set the people against us, and now you can't control them."

"They lied to you," I replied. "You're dealing with a slander."

"They told us . . ." he stammered, upset.

"Don't pay any attention to what they say. I came to defend you, and I am ready for anything, provided not one more drop of blood is shed."

The young man fell silent. Don Ulises had got up and was looking out at the highway through the half-raised blinds.

"They'll get their just deserts," he growled, and letting the blinds drop, he ordered his son: "Tell them to take away the gas tanks, and you yourself cut off the electricity."

"Leave the house, Don Ulises. I'll go with you in your truck. It's your last chance."

He hesitated for a second.

"No," he said, "I'm not the man to run away."

"Forget your pride, and *think*. Nothing can be done with angry people."

"You're wasting your time. Now what has to come will come."

Although he was making an effort to maintain his prideful reputation, his eyes betrayed him. I saw in them a certain anxiety, an insecurity that he was trying to control as he rose continually to his feet or attended to trifling details, while his house was surrounded by ten thousand enraged men.

Behind him, pistol in hand, was Adalberto, his chief gunman, not taking his eyes from his master. A little thread of blood trickled out of his hair and, sliding down his forehead, was staining his white shirt.

"You're still bleeding, Adalberto," the boss said. "Go get my wife to take care of it."

"I don't want to leave you, Don Ulises."

"Go, and come right back. The priest will take your place. Wouldn't you like to handle a gun?"

I left my seat and went to the leaded-glass roof. Through the peacocks and roses on the glass, Don Ulises's real peacocks spread their silky tails among the flowers in the garden.

"You must decide," I told him without turning round.

"Are you admiring my peacocks?"

"I am admiring the criminal indifference with which you doom your family."

Adalberto's cold voice was heard:

"Don Ulises, they're burning the south wing of the saw-mill!"

The boss went out without saying a word, and I remained alone. Tinged with scarlet and yellow lights, people were moving about among the peacock tails. A muffled roar which I might have taken for distant thunder made the porcelain figurines vibrate in their glass cabinets.

"What must I do?" I asked myself anxiously. I saw the clouds of their hate gathering, and I stood leaning my forehead on the glass, but no idea occurred to me.

Father Suárez touched me on the shoulder.

"What shall we do, señor cura?" he asked, guessing my in-decision.

"I'll answer you quite frankly: I don't know. Have you thought of anything?"

"Do leave this house. It will soon be burning on all sides."

"Perhaps it may be better to persuade the besiegers than to help the besieged. Come with me, father. It will be a terrible fight."

The decision had been made. Was it the best one? The most prudent one? Should I have stayed in the house and defended its owners tooth and nail? What drove me to leave? Could I trust in being obeyed? Was my power so great that I was going to achieve a miracle?

41

Above the stairs loomed piles of planks and the machine shed enveloped in smoke from the fire. I went quickly down the stairs. Two servant girls, accompanied by María, were carry-ing water, and I heard the neighing of a horse trapped in his stable, mingled with cries and the noise of shots.

"They are shooting," I said to myself. "They are shooting, and it does not matter to them if they fire at their priest. My God, enlighten me, have mercy upon us."

At the exit gate a little boy caught me by the cassock.

"Señor cura, help me get my bicycle out. It's the only one I have."

The bicycle was a short distance away, surrounded by flames. I was rolling up the sleeves of my cassock when Father Suárez stepped forward and, clearing the flames in one leap, took the bicycle and rode it back across the burning barrier like a bolt of lightning.

In the street now a machine-gun burst sounded behind us, and I instinctively sought the refuge of the wall.

"What is this, father? Are they shooting at us?"

Father Suárez's pallor frightened me.

He murmured in a faint voice:

"They've hit me."

"Where?" I cried, shaking his shoulder.

"Here," he went on, holding out his right hand.

I examined it curiously. A stone fragment kicked up by a bullet had caused a deep wound above his thumb.

I took out my handkerchief and, making a bandage of it, calmed him.

"It's only a scratch. It will be well tomorrow."

"Señor cura, let me go back to the rectory. I must not expose myself. I am supporting my mother and sisters, and if I were to fail them . . ."

"But you exposed yourself to fire saving a bicycle, and now you're afraid!"

"A burn is not death," he went on mildly.

My indignation was quieted.

"Go to the Red Cross. You'll be safer there."

He kissed my hand and went off with long strides. I had arrived at the corner where the Indian died. His two burros, laden with pots, indifferent to the excitement, wandered along the street looking for the sparse grass growing in the cracks between the stones.

Father Villaverde, another of my vicars, joined me.

"Father, I need a microphone to talk to the people. Otherwise I'll be in danger of not being heard."

"It's not easy to find any just now, but I'll try to get one," the father replied.

From the mountain and the upper districts men and women were coming down in waves. Their children, dragging along, crossed the street and sought refuge among the trees in the center strip, or rolled up garbage cans full of stones and protected themselves behind those improvised trenches.

The fear of being shot at without shelter kept the front of

Don Ulises's home clear, and people gathered on the corners and on the rooftops, or moved from one side to the other carrying daggers, rifles, pistols, and bottles filled with gasoline.

The situation at that time was very different from the one I had left. While I was in Don Ulises's house, people had run home to get weapons. Hunting rifles, antique pistols, daggers, and even knives came out of their hiding places in a moment. The problem of ammunition was partly resolved by looting the only store selling cartridges—the old proprietor reported the scene to me afterward, peering at me over his blurred glasses and raising his hands to his bald head—and they provided themselves with gasoline by emptying automobile tanks and attacking gasoline stations.

That agitation, apparently confused and lacking a plan, obeyed its own laws. The boss's rule was like a wound, and the leucocytes were moving in in order to combat the infection and exterminate it. Everywhere they were improvising "Molotov cocktails," that is, bottles equipped with a wick and filled with gasoline. Young girls contributed their handkerchiefs, and I saw a barefoot girl take off her shawl and offer it to make wicks.

I remember a little ragamuffin (he would not have been more than twelve) who passed in front of me holding a tiny pistol.

"What are you doing here?" I asked him, catching him by his shirt.

He answered me with the utmost dignity:

"I am defending the fatherland, señor cura."

Several students approached a young policeman who was standing by the fire, leaning on his gun.

"We have to break down the boss's door," they told him. "See if you can hit the lock."

Obediently, the young man grasped his weapon and shot at the door, without hitting the target. I was a short distance away, struggling with a vendor from the market, and I could not have prevented him, but as soon as I was free, I spoke to the policeman.

"You're doing wrong. They commanded you to keep order, and you're doing the opposite of what they commanded."

He looked at me in astonishment.

"The president sent me to take care of the interests of the people, and I shot at the house of their principal enemy!"

How could I make that policeman understand the concept of order? For him, as for thousands of men, the boss was the enemy, the principal cause of all their ills, and he considered it a duty, even an urgent duty, to contribute to his destruction. They had set him up as the defender of the people, as the avenger of their wrongs, and this conviction conferred a dignity upon him and made his eyes shine with a clear light, looking straight ahead.

The change that had been wrought—and God forgive me this evil thought—drew thousands of men out of the sleep in which they lay, out of their daily death, and made them feel so intensely and profoundly alive that their strength was transformed into something tangible, like the loud, majestic wind that rises on summer nights, sweeping the earth to make it worthy to receive the purifying water of the rain.

I waited in vain for the microphone to arrive. Father Villaverde found the sound truck in the street, abandoned and minus the key, and there was no use knocking at the stores and houses that remained closed and silent.

"Go back!" I cried. "Go back! They are better armed, and you'll be the ones to get killed!"

For ten minutes, or an hour (for I had lost the conception of time), I fought resolutely, snatching away their weapons and incendiary bottles, or exerting myself to persuade them to return home. Here I grabbed a dagger, there a pistol; a few steps farther on I managed to get hold of a couple of bombs or a knife, to no effect, because dozens and dozens of incendiary bottles, shots, and stones were raining onto the house from all directions, and my efforts were completely useless.

The pockets of my cassock, full of weapons, weighed me down, and the shouting drowned out my cries. I tried to reason. My error, as I see it now, consisted of leaving Don Ulises's house, of not assessing my weakness in the face of the people's anger, and I decided to return, disregarding bullets or incendiary bombs. Lifting my cassock I ran across the highway, but I had not reached the center strip when a handful of bold men set out to follow me and, surrounding me, obliged me to retreat, this time by force.

"Where are you going?" they asked, panting.

"I must save them! I must save them all! The soldiers from Zitácuaro will soon be here."

"Let them come," they replied. "We'll welcome them with shots."

From that moment I was, in fact, kidnapped. Four or five men, among whom I distinguished a gigantic blacksmith who had been entrusted with repairs to the church, watched my slightest movements. The restriction infuriated me.

"Francisco, I *have* to go to that house even though you oppose me."

Francisco took my arm.

"No, señor cura, don't move from here, I beg you."

"Take your hands off! You're committing a big sin."

The giant's eyes, abashed like those of a child, looked at me imploringly.

"Have pity on me, señor cura. I don't want to hurt you."

42

The impending massacre was put off. Apparently the boss and his gunmen were not firing now. Flames were borne above the sawmill, and smoke began to issue from the broken windows.

I could not stop thinking about Don Ulises. He could be plotting one of his *coups,* one of his rash surprises, and allowing time for the soldiers to come from Zitácuaro—it was only half an hour away by the highway—or from the city of Morelia.

The fire added to the sultry midday heat. The distant trees blended stickily, and a thick haze covered the woods and spread across the ash gray roofs. I do not know where the millions of flies had come from. They hovered in little eddies, clinging intolerably to our greasy skins bathed in sweat.

It was an immense crowd. They had gathered not only on the corners, on the rooftops and balconies, but also in the neighboring streets. Hundreds of palm hats and heads covered with shawls shifted rapidly or grouped themselves in compact, uniform masses.

People continued to surround me, and women clung hysterically to my cassock.

"For the love of God, for the love of God," they begged, their empty brains reverting to a form devoid of meaning at that time.

Shots rang out everywhere. Muffled detonations opened a hollow space in the midst of the vibrant shouting, a hole of silence which the distant rattle of machine guns and the wail of the siren afterward filled.

43

While I was struggling, confused, the shouting, the shots, the thud of stones falling, the running and exclamations ceased, and I heard a strident burst of laughter like the neighing of a herd of frightened horses, the sound of all the windows in the world being broken at once, an atrocious frightening laugh, which came out of ten thousand throats and which I could only compare with the laughter that those condemned to hell will produce on the day of the Last Judgment.

I was free, and I ran to the front of the house. I could see nothing unusual. Smoke issued from the windows, and bullet holes stained the yellow painted façade. People were running in all directions, drunkenly jumping for joy, raising their arms and exclaiming, swamped by a wave of madness:

"He's dead! The boss is dead! Tajimaroa is free! Our slavery is over!"

Women were embracing each other sobbing or, joining hands, were dancing. Men emerged from behind the garbage cans, swung down from the rooftops and shouted, continued to shout, frantic to be free, with that savage joy which otherwise would have made them explode in the air.

Don Ulises's body was lying face up, stretched out on the sidewalk, his feet on the sill of his half-open door. He must have died instantly. Whitish matter swimming in viscous liquid appeared in his hair, and his face, a brutal face which death had not softened, was covered with blood. His right hand, still clenched, was reaching toward the machine gun he had dropped when he fell, and it was found a short distance away. Flies were swarming on his soft flesh and drinking from the pool of blood congealing on the sidewalk.

Hundreds of men approached the body, fascinated. They looked at it as one looks at a recently killed tiger, still warm, and some poked it with their foot, fearful that it might be going to get up. Only then did I notice that I had left behind in his house my satchel with the stole, crucifix, and holy oils, and there was nothing else to do but to begin softly saying the prayer for the dead.

The townsfolk were arriving in ever-greater numbers. The fascination that the slain man had produced in them was weakening, while their wrath, momentarily appeased, was increasing, and the desire for revenge took hold of them once more.

I went on praying, but my voice was drowned in their shouts.

"We ought to drag him off."

"Let's drag him! That way he'll pay for his crimes."

The idea that his body was going to be desecrated, that I should be present at its debasement, prompted me to react.

"Don't touch him!" I shouted, beside myself. "That man is already judged by God!"

Why did I utter that cry? Because I was defending Don Ulises dead, though I had not defended him even when there had been time to save his life? Was it not hatred, repressed rage against the boss, an unconscious desire for revenge that paralyzed me, reducing me to impotence? I had been a plaything in the hands of the crowd, an indecisive, intimidated man, but suddenly I recovered my will and straightened up ready to fight for their victim, for the remains of a man overcome by the violence against which I had thought I was fighting, although in reality I was a part of it.

Naturally I made no such reflections to myself. Dramatic events were rushing rapidly upon us all, and I was far from thinking at that time that my conduct would be causing me acute remorse.

Hearing my cry, the crowd began to move back and leave me alone with the dead man on the blackened sidewalk, carpeted with glass and bits of plaster.

"Call the Red Cross to pick up the body," I ordered.

Then the door was opened, and María, stepping over her father's body, faced the crowd that had been momentarily calmed.

"Cowards! What more do you want? What are you waiting for? To kill all of us? Here I am! Finish us all at once! Cowards, cowards!"

Her voice sounded strident. Her small figure dressed in black brought to mind Don Ulises's phrase: "They are good women and good Mexicans." María stood in the middle of the highway, her hands clenched, her hair disheveled. Her upper lip, shadowed by a dark down, was lifted, revealing her teeth, and her appearance vaguely suggested that of a little hunted animal that had suddenly decided to defend itself.

I ran toward her.

"María! Go back to your mother! Don't foolishly expose yourself to death!"

She did not hear me. Turning to the crowd, she went on shouting:

"Cowards! Cowards!"

A shot rang out. The woman raised her hands to her breast and moaned:

"I'm wounded!"

"Can you walk?" I asked, supporting her around the waist. "I think so."

I held her up as far as the door, and María entered the house, her legs trembling, holding to the walls for support.

44

As soon as she disappeared, I heard new exclamations:

"Don Ulises's peacocks! Don Ulises's peacocks!"

Mad with terror, the birds had left their garden refuge and were flying, or rather, gliding in the greasy air, their thin necks extended, their cackling muffled. It could not be called flight. Rather, it was a spasm, a leap into the air, an animal instinct in the presence of death, a sluggish flight that destroyed the image of serenity, elegance, and vanity they symbolized. They flew. They scratched the air. They rose and fell over an enemy garden where the roses might have been changed into greedy hands, into flowers with five pistils, flowers with pink, sticky calixes that opened and waved with a man-eating voracity.

Two peacocks, excited by the shouting, managed to find safety on a nearby rooftop. The third slowly planed, passed near me, and landed beside the boss's body tumbled on the sidewalk. I could not avoid a cold shudder. Its feet, its thin, ugly scaly feet, stepped in the pool of blood, and its open beak, its open, eager beak—recognizing him, sniffing him, like a blind man's cane—touched the wounds, the spilled material of thought, the ruined cells that had contained experience, memories, deceits, instincts, loves, hates, pride. It had all disappeared. His mouth did not speak the customary words; with his spirit had escaped the secret of their coded language, and he was only a lukewarm prey on which the flies were cruelly buzzing. The great bird seemed to understand the change that had been worked upon its master. It uttered a long, laborious caw and slowly, heavily resumed its flight, turning toward the crowd that was awaiting its prey. Still its enameled tail, its silky tail sown with iridescent eyes, its tail that would unfold in the rose garden with the sound of an enormous fan, glittered, shone for a moment, recovered its old balance, but two hundred hands seized it and picked its feathers by the handful. Then the crowd opened up, left an empty space, and at the feet of the people I could see the great bird white, naked, degraded, like a ghost of itself, like the very figure of the arrogant man who lay there on a tapestry of glass, his hand stretched out, reaching desperately and vainly toward his silent machine gun.

45

The Red Cross aides appeared at last. People kept back from the corpse and remained quiet while they lifted Don Ulises's body onto the stretcher. I crossed his arms over his breast, and since Father Villaverde had returned without the microphone, said to him:

"Father, you go with the body to the Ayuntamiento, and you're to answer to me that nothing unpleasant happens on the way."

The body (I must say it to absolve my parishioners) was not dragged with a rope, nor was it an object of profanation, as the newspapers reported the next day. According to Father

Villaverde's report, seeing Don Ulises's head waver because of the movement of the stretcher, people remarked incredulously: "He's alive! He didn't die, as they made us believe," but this was due to the idea that the people had formed of the boss's invincible power. Many were convinced that he wore a bulletproof vest, and the most incredulous thought that he was pretending to be dead and that it was all just a trick. Don Ulises represented the all-powerful force against which they had struggled for thirty years, and his unexpected death, his destruction, occurring in the very moment their battle began, was a fact that plunged them into the greatest confusion.

His head kept shifting with the swaying of the stretcher, and people ran behind, exclaiming fearfully:

"He's alive! He's alive! The priest deceived us!"

Father Villaverde had them halt and, turning to the crowd:

"Look at him. Look at him closely. He is dead."

46

As well as I can reconstruct it for Your Grace, the situation inside the house was extremely serious. With Don Ulises struck down on his very doorstep—some say he died because he rashly insisted on going out into the street, and others speak of a willful sacrifice—Adalberto, the only man beside him, tried to get him into the house, taking hold of his feet, but the rain of bullets prevented him, and he had to turn back. Doña Paula called to her husband from the courtyard:

"Dear, come with us. Dear . . ."

Adalberto appeared at the top of the stairway with an altered face.

"They've killed the master," was all he could say.

The elderly woman rushed headlong down the stairs sobbing:

"Dear, my dear . . ."

Young Ulises put his arms around his mother.

"Don't lose your head, Mamá. Keep calm."

The woman fought, struggling to escape.

"Let me go," she said between sobs. "I want to die with my dear."

"Go to bed, rest," Ulises urged her as he carried her to a room on the lower floor where his wife, his four children and his sister María had already gathered.

Adalberto had returned to the salon with the fixed idea of rescuing the body of his chief, but the gunmen were fighting apart in the sawmill.

He had scarcely entered the room when the young man heard an imperious voice asking from the stairs:

"Are you there, Ulises?"

He looked out of the window and saw a group of twenty men, armed with pistols and daggers, who had got into the house by taking advantage of the confusion outside.

Without saying a word, he picked up his rifle and waited.

"Are you there, Ulises?" the voice asked again, more arrogantly.

Their faces contorted by hate, the men began slowly to descend the stairs. Ulises thought of his mother with her heart trouble, of his children, of his wounded sister, and decided to answer, knowing beforehand what awaited him.

"Yes, I'm here. What do you want of me?"

Controlling her grief, Doña Paula tried to defend her son.

"All of Ulises Roca's family is here. Finish with us all at once."

"Come out of that room, Ulises, or we'll drag you out by force," the voice ordered. "No one will harm you at all."

His mother tried to stop Ulises.

"Don't go. It's better to die all together."

"Mother," the young man pleaded, "I must go. They promised not to hurt me."

Disengaging himself from Doña Paula's arms, he left the

room, unarmed, and the men surrounded him. Now at the street door, in the same place where Don Ulises had fallen, the sight of his son revived people's anger, that unreasoning anger which strikes blindly without knowing what it strikes, and in a moment they had knocked him to the ground, stabbed him with their daggers.

I had been twenty yards away, watching the departure of the stretcher, and the young man's cries made me run to the door. Ulises was lying unconscious in the reddish pool left by his father. He gave the impression of being dead. His face, disfigured by the wounds, ran with blood which was spreading rapidly over his sport shirt, and flames from the gasoline had burned his hair and were beginning to burn his trousers. I threw myself upon him and with the edges of my cassock managed to put out the fire.

Infuriated, I drove back his assailants, shouting at them with all my strength:

"Ulises is innocent, and Christians don't murder the innocent!"

I remember only that the men retreated. The crowd stopped, falling back expectantly. I stayed beside Ulises. It was impossible to recognize in him the proud young man who had pointed his rifle at me, accusing me of setting the people against his family. His face—they had broken his dark glasses—disappeared under a black mask, and his shirt was burned and blood-stained.

Kneeling, I began the response, not taking my eyes from the people:

"*Liberame Domine, de morte aeterna, in die illa tremenda, quando coeli movendi sunt et terra. Dum veneris judicare saeculum per ignem.*"

Through the haze I saw the crowd keeping calm and silent, and I heard nothing but the din of the fire like a roar behind me.

"*Dies illa, dies irae, calamitatis et miseriae, dies magna et amara valde. Dum veneris judicare saeculum per ignem.*"

The day of wrath, of calamity, and misery, the great bitter day when the Lord could come to judge the world by fire, had arrived. The people did not understand the meaning of my words, but they guessed that they somehow had a bearing on the crimes committed by all of them, and that in that terrible hour they were achieving an expiation ordained by the Divinity. They remained silent and removed their hats, but no one was kneeling, and their desire for revenge still fought with their piety and refused to retreat.

"*Requiem aeternam dona eis Domine; et lux perpetua luceat eis.*"

The crowd fell on its knees in an undulating motion, like a high tide falling on the beach, and the potent murmur of the prayer made the hot, sticky air vibrate.

Had I needed to crawl naked and powerless for all my fifty years just in order to be present at that scene? They listened to my words as to the rain, a rain that erased the blood and quenched their thirst for vengeance, a rain that was the sign of forgiveness, the sign that the wrath of God had been satisfied with the tyrant's death, and that the day of wrath, of calamity, and misery had come to its end.

Perhaps, Monsignor, that moment of exaltation was nothing but a fit of pride, of devilish pride. The Lord returned to me the power he had bestowed upon me on the day of my ordination in order to hurl me again into impotence, to make me understand that His designs are unfathomable and that no sinner may feel himself to be the instrument of divine will.

The prayer was nearing its end, and with it the miracle was fading. The Red Cross aides had returned and were waiting for it to conclude, kneeling beside the stretcher. Ulises came out of his faint. He opened his eyes, tried to move; the crowd got to its feet, and I heard their angry cries again.

"Ulises," I said in his ear, "don't move, or they'll kill you."

No doubt he understood my warning, because he held himself rigid, and I myself helped them to lift him onto the stretcher. Father Villaverde accompanied him, carrying a crucifix in his hand.

"Pray, father," I begged him as he set out, "pray so that everyone can hear you."

"You may rest assured, señor cura. I will answer for his life."

47

Don Ulises's relatives and the gunmen remained to be saved. I returned to the house, crossing the salon quickly. Neither curtains nor rugs were left; the pianola was burning slowly; the decapitated head of a statue was supported on the edge of a broken window, and the roof was only a pile of twisted iron.

The gunmen had gathered in the downstairs room where the boss's family still remained. Sitting on a bed, Ulises's wife was nursing her small son. None of the children was crying. The older ones stayed in one corner, not understanding what was happening, and a little girl of three was lulling her doll to sleep, singing softly, while the gunmen, their weapons cocked, mounted guard at the window.

Doña Paula was busy bandaging María's shoulder, and as I entered, she regarded me with reddened eyes.

"What has become of Ulises, señor cura? Did they kill him?"

"Ulises is safe at the Red Cross."

"You are trying to console me."

"I'm telling you the truth, and you must believe me."

"Oh, father," she exclaimed, "what a great misfortune has fallen on our family!"

"Let us leave," I said to her, taking her by the hand. "Here, we are all in great danger."

"Why leave? They'll kill us in the street."

"No one will do anything to you, I assure you," and taking

one of the little girls in my arms, I started toward the door.

The family's appearance was received with whistles and shouts. María drew back, and her small chin trembled as her father's had trembled in the sawmill. The child Ulises's wife was carrying began to cry. Doña Paula, throwing back her shawl from her head, stepped forward with her arms outstretched.

"Isn't the evil you have done us enough for you? Aren't you satisfied?"

This elderly woman's dignity and nobility, her words that held no rancor, calmed the people. We crossed the highway in silence, and the family took refuge, unmolested, in the house opposite, where some of their relatives lived.

48

In the Ayuntamiento things were not going any better. Of the twelve inexperienced policemen, six had been detailed to Don Ulises's house, and the other six, charged with guarding the rooftop, thought they were obliged to shoot in the air from time to time to answer the shots that, coming from undetermined locations, missed their mark on the façade of the run-down building.

The mayor was a prisoner in his own office. The crowd was watching his every movement through the windows and circulating through the corridors, anxious to view the body of its enemy.

Owing to a strange coincidence that canceled out Manuel's victory and the boss's defeat, their two bodies lay on adjacent stretchers, while the body of the Indian was set aside at one end of the corridor, and no one paid any attention to it.

Those remains, far from appeasing the ones who had not taken part in the assault on the house, inflamed them. They too were demanding their own victims, they wanted to contribute to the destruction of the boss's rule, and their anger, lacking an outlet until then, was directed toward the jail located in one corner of the courtyard, where Avelino remained confined.

The jail was not an easy one to take. A thick-barred grating adequately protected the prisoners, and in the mayor's office were present, in addition to the warden, the commandant of police, two soldiers armed with rifles, and Father Miranda, one of my vicars whom I had stationed at the Red Cross.

At three o'clock in the afternoon, five hundred people—the majority of them women—met in front of the jail, begging for Avelino to be delivered to them. The warden, a nervous little man with curly hair, feverish eyes and a prominent Adam's apple, whom the flame of civic oratory was devouring, had thought it would be easy to control the infuriated crowd. He went to the door, raised his weak, trembling hand, but before he had finished opening his mouth, the crowd dragged him inside, and his voice was heard declaiming "Dear fellow citizens," "Dear fellow citizens" above the insults and cries of the women who shouted:

"Throw him out! He's a murderer!"

"Give us the key. We want the key, not your stupid speeches."

Father Miranda intervened, protecting the frightened warden.

"Get back, get back! He doesn't have the key."

The women were the ones who were most excited. There the old women of the town had gathered, the Furies, the Gorgons of whom I spoke to Your Grace. They had spent a great part of their lives sitting on the sidewalk or on the floor in the marketplace, selling toasted seeds or some other inferior merchandise, and from below, from that level where beggars and starving dogs wander, they had watched the fat commandant who ate their fruit and walked beside them caressing the girls and making fun of the men.

Paz, the illiterate old woman to whom one of her grand-

children had described the way in which two companions
had fallen poisoned beside the blackboard at school, cap-
tained the mob.

"Let's pull out the whole bush," she howled. "Let's not
leave a single one alive."

Father Miranda, a man at the peak of his strength, helped
by the commandant and the soldiers, managed to clear the
warden's office, and the uproar appeared to be checked.

Ten minutes later hundreds of men and women rushed
headlong at the office again, swept away the defenders—
Father Miranda momentarily lost consciousness as the result
of a blow—and the grating was wrenched from its frame,
the thick bars bent and Avelino dragged out into the courtyard.

As they passed close to Don Ulises's body, the group
stopped, and one man said:

"Look, there's your father. That's how you're going to
die."

Making a desperate effort, Avelino threw himself to the
ground and managed to elude them. The muscular man with
his broad head was reduced to only an instinct fighting to
protect its life. He escaped from the outstretched hands,
rolled on the ground and shook himself, frantically repelling
the men who tried to capture him.

One woman hit him on the head with a stick, and Avelino
fell. Another Fury then jumped on him and, beating him in
the face with a large stone, cried:

"This is for my son that you murdered!"

"Never have I seen anything like it," Father Miranda remarked. "Avelino reminded me of an insect, one of those
insects we mutilate when we are children and are practicing
our first cruelty, an insect whose mutilation bestows a sacred
character upon it, a force beyond the organic, which wakes
our piety and our homicidal fury, our repugnance and our
anxiety to end the agony, the monstrous suffering, of that
fly without feet and wings, that headless worm, those grass-

hoppers deprived of their eyes and antennae, of that blind, crazy Avelino, in short, without any other reaction than the elemental one of finding a safe place for himself."

He uttered a shout:

"No, I don't want to die!"

Father Miranda forced his way through and reached the battered man. It was too late. Avelino lay on the ground, already dead, but his body, obedient to his appeal for life, to his last cry, went on twitching convulsively.

49

In the same room on the lower floor where the family had sought refuge, Don Ulises's men were finding themselves trapped. Not all of them had been his gunmen. One of them, an old man, was the watchman at the sawmill; another was a member of the town council, who had visited the house that morning for the purpose of settling certain land matters and had joined the boss's forces; the other six—among whom were Adalberto and the deposed mayor, Guadalupe Cielo— were gunmen, old-time policemen and the boss's trusted men.

The sawmill was burning furiously. The upper floor was also on fire, and the windows were exploding, covering the stairs with broken glass. My cassock was torn and scorched, and although I had taken off my clerical collar and perspiration had relieved me somewhat, the little room with its over-heated walls was the nearest thing to an oven that I could imagine. Furthermore, the incendiary bottles continued to rain down, and the shouting in the street was increasing.

The eight men—with the exception of Adalberto and Guadalupe, who had not lost their composure—had an altered look, and they paced the room in long strides or looked nervously out of the narrow window.

"Nothing will happen to you, men, if you follow my in-

structions. Put down your weapons and sit on the floor.
You'll be in less danger that way."

"I'd rather die killing somebody," Adalberto answered,
regarding me distrustfully.

"Your stubbornness isn't endangering just you; it's endangering all your companions."

"With Don Ulises dead, nothing matters to me."

"He died because he had a machine gun in his hand."

"I'm the one responsible for his death. I shouldn't have
let him go out," he exclaimed, and turning, went into a bathroom next door.

The watchman sat down on the floor and began saying
his rosary. I was reminded of my father. So he had sat, his
head bent and his eyes closed, while outside we heard the
shouts and blasphemies of the combatants. I approached him
and, putting my hand on his coarse gray hair, told him:

"Pray. Your prayer will do us all good."

Three of the gunmen dropped their weapons on the bed
and sat down beside the watchman. Suffocated, almost gasp-
ing, I went to the door. The dividing wall was being pierced
in three or four places and, judging from the force of the
blows, the assailants would not be long in storming our last
redoubt. I went back into the room, worried. Except for
Guadalupe, who was still on his feet, the rest were sitting on
the floor, and their rifles and pistols were piled on the bed.

Adalberto, recovered now, came out of the bathroom, went
to the window and observed the progress of the demolition,
not letting go of his pistol.

"You see that, señor cura?" he asked in a calm voice.
"They're bent on murdering us."

"What will you gain by killing a hundred men? They're
ten thousand, and you're not even a dozen."

"You, señor cura, want to deliver us bound hand and foot
to our enemies."

Shrinking from my glance, Guadalupe turned to Adalberto.

"You're right. He stirred people up against Don Ulises. He wants to surrender us, no less."

"You don't know what my real intentions are."

"I've been the municipal president, and I know you well, but this time you won't succeed in deceiving us."

Breached at last, the wall showed two large gaps, and eight or ten men appeared in the dust from the falling bricks. I stood on the threshold with my arms crossed. Seeing me, they halted, surprised.

"Get out of the doorway, señor cura," said a butcher with a large moustache. "This is no place for you."

"Where do you think a priest should be?"

"With the people, not with the people's murderers."

"You have no right to judge or condemn anyone. I stand with the weak, with the few, not with the many, and it is my duty to prevent you from burdening your consciences with a new crime."

"Let's not argue," said the butcher. "You're a priest. When you get slapped, you advise turning the other cheek."

A one-eyed man, scarred by smallpox, spit scornfully on the ground.

"He can watch the boss killing his parishioners without saying a word, but he's horrified when we avenge our dead."

"Shout. Get it out of your system. Insult me today," I replied, becoming wrought up. "Tomorrow you'll thank me for what I'm doing for you. Don't you forget it."

The work of sapping was finished. A piece of wall fell on the ground. Through the gap appeared the head of the horse Don Ulises used to ride. A rope held him by the neck, and the animal looked at us with his large frightened eyes, beseeching help.

"The horse!" exclaimed the attackers. "It's Don Ulises's white horse!"

"He bought it with our money," wailed the one-eyed man, "with what he stole from us."

Three shots rang out, the horse reared stiffly, showing its

yellow teeth, and before the dust had settled, we had a good
handful of men facing us. I thought I recognized them. Hate
is an ecstasy too, a madness that opens mouths and distends
them, closes eyelids, leaving a slit through which a sharp
glassy light appears, and clenches hands, as they are clenched
when they beg a pardon or a favor from the bottom of an
exasperated heart. They wore the same old faded sheepskin
jackets, their shirts were dirty and their trousers well patched,
but those familiar garments covered a few men who, despite
all their similarities, were not now the men whose humble
faces I was used to seeing from the altar through candlelight
and incense smoke.

50

I confess to Your Grace that I was not afraid. It was something worse: the certainty that the Lord had taken away my
power, and that the miracle worked a few minutes ago would
not be repeated. "The struggle is coming," I told myself,
"the physical battle—the blows, death, desecration, degrada-
tion." They were moving forward. They were advancing,
their ghostly faces covered with dust, their eyes flashing. A
stocky artisan with curly hair took me by the shoulder.

"Stand aside, señor cura."

"You shan't come in!" I cried, shaking him off. "These
men are in sanctuary. Do you hear? They're in sanctuary."

Ten hands took hold of my cassock, dragging me away from
the door. Unexpectedly, Father Suárez intervened and, using
an energy of which I would not have believed him capable,
forced the attackers to retreat.

I looked at him gratefully.

"Father," I told him, "you came at the right time!"

His unbandaged hand was still bleeding. His curly hair
was sticking to his forehead, and a surprising strength had
taken possession of his tough thin body.

The men had retreated to the hedge. A young man cried: "Don Ulises accused us of being a town full of chickens. The time has come to show we are not, to finish with that viper's nest!"

"Come on if you dare," Father Suárez exploded, addressing the youth, "but by yourself."

"Take off your cassock," the young man answered, taking a step forward, "and fight like a man."

The father removed his cassock and, before I could prevent it, flattened the young man with a sudden blow to the jaw.

His ideas about priests must have undergone something of a change. Instead of proffering both cheeks, Father Suárez put his enemy *hors de combat* with a blow that might have made his seminary gymnasium teacher proud, and to my surprise, his use of violence, far from inciting them, calmed them down.

51

It was five o'clock in the afternoon. In the sawmill the rest of the lumber was burning, and flames from the blaze rose and were mixed with the reddish glare of twilight.

Below, the smoke and dust of the demolition partly hid the ruined wall. New attackers leaped through the openings and, joining the earlier ones, they gestured and shouted without persuading themselves to launch a second attack.

"We must stand fast," I told Father Suárez, who had put on his cassock again. "The soldiers ordered from Zitácuaro will be here shortly, and this nightmare will be over."

"I'm worried only about your forgiving me."

"Forgiving you? What must I forgive you?"

"I deserted you in the hour of danger."

"Let's not talk about that any more," I told him, hiding my emotion and returning to the room.

Aside from the elderly watchman who remained seated, the seven men, no doubt spurred on by Guadalupe, were grouped at the window, their pistols and rifles ready.

"Don't I deserve your trust yet?" I asked, turning to face Guadalupe. "Don't you think I am ready to defend you with my life, if necessary?"

"You I trust, señor cura, but not those cowards."

He was perfectly calm. He spoke coldly, not allowing any emotion to show. His index finger rested on the trigger, and his telescopic rifle seemed to form part of his muscular body.

"Blood blinds men," he went on thoughtfully in an aside. "I know that from experience."

Nothing could alarm me so much as that decision against which neither arguments nor entreaties prevailed. The man had to choose between dying like Avelino and dying while defending himself, and he had resolved the dilemma beforehand. From his enemies he could expect neither charity nor pity. They were judging the gunmen without discrimination, and in their innermost heart they had condemned him to death. They needed only to carry out the verdict.

"Look at them," said the mayor. "Here they come."

A numerous group of thirty or forty men were resolutely approaching the room. Accompanied by Father Suárez, I went out to meet them.

"Stop, in the name of God! What else do you want?"

"We want the boss's thugs," the butcher answered. "That's what we want."

"Not all of these are his bodyguards, and if some of them are guilty, justice will take care of them."

"Let the thugs come out. We don't care about the others."

"They'll not come out. They're in my custody."

"We're sorry for your sake, señor cura. We've waited too long already."

Adalberto came noiselessly out of the room and planted himself in front of them.

"I was Don Ulises's chief bodyguard," he said simply, by way of introduction.

The one-eyed man raised his pistol, uttering a curse, but before he had time to shoot, he fell to the ground.

I heard Guadalupe exclaim from the window:

"If you don't get back, I'll kill all of you! That was only a warning."

As if crazed, the men threw themselves upon Father Suárez, who was blocking their way, and I ran to his defense.

I did not expect help from anyone. The power had gone out of me, and I was alone, with no other strength than the primitive, elemental one of anger. Panting, clenching my teeth and fists, I struggled frantically, seizing the attackers by their hair and throwing them to the ground, stamping on them, drunk with a savage frenzy, until I felt myself falling into a well of shadows, into an abyss where the darkness was so thick that I seemed to float and sink into it without ever reaching the bottom of that chasm.

When I opened my eyes, the first thing I saw was a steel helmet and, below it, the face of a captain bending over me. I felt very weak, and the left side of my jaw was aching.

The captain got up, saying to me:

"What a blow they gave you, señor cura!"

"Yes, captain," I replied, rubbing my cheek, "it was a lightning knockout. Are Don Ulises's men safe?"

"They're over there. We came in time to save them."

"No," Adalberto interposed, "the priest's decision saved us."

"Anyhow, they escaped with their lives. That's the important thing."

"We received orders scarcely an hour ago to come to Tajimaroa," the officer said by way of excuse.

"If you will permit, I should like to leave."

"Go along, señor cura. You've borne yourself like a brave man."

"I'm not sorry for what has happened, but neither am I glad about it. It's a sad victory."

Outside in the streets and in the plaza invaded by the shadows of the night, the crowd was breaking up. Cordons of soldiers protected the Ayuntamiento where—so they told me—the state's attorney, just arrived from Morelia, had set up his court.

We were emerging from anonymity. We heard the artificial, mechanical radio voices broadcasting Boss Ulises Roca's death "at the hands of the maddened people," and a continuous stream of photographers, cameramen, and journalists came climbing out of their automobiles, eager for sensational news. Our only hotel was inadequate to hold all the secret police, lawyers, and politicians who descended upon Tajimaroa.

I crossed the garden of the atrium where only the hushed cries of the owls were heard. My little cloister, abandoned since morning, was silent and dark. I sat down without turning on the light, as on other nights when the thought of Don Ulises had tormented me to no avail. Now, for the first time, he no longer existed, and I must reflect upon the meaning of his violent death, answer the questions the journalists and court people were asking me, but I was unable to coordinate my ideas. As in a lightning flash I had seen the people exercising their justice, or rather, I had looked upon the shining face of their victory, but behind that victory that had no banners, no songs for their regained liberty, no laurel wreaths for the tyrant-killers, there remained a trail of death, a few ashes drenched with blood and tears, a few guilty or innocent victims.

Each bastille—and it was legitimate, Monsignor, to consider Don Ulises's home as a small bastille—has been won by killing, because despots do not hear the voices of those they subjugate, do not voluntarily abandon their power, and it is necessary to destroy them in order to destroy the power they embody, and their victims, those cold, grotesque vic-

tims, those corpses swollen and riddled with bullets, are their
tokens and trophies of victory, the tribute people must pay
for the right to plant their justice on the stage of the world
or in the forgotten country town of Tajimaroa.

52

At eleven o'clock at night, the solemn, even somewhat ig-
noble faces of two secret police looked in at the rectory, announcing that they had orders to take me before the state's
attorney.

"No, señor cura," Father Suárez said vehemently, "you
mustn't go alone. The time has come for reprisals, and it's
not improbable that they might accuse you of having stirred
up our parishioners. I've heard some rumors to that effect."

"We'll all go together," proposed Father Villaverde.

"I shall go alone, and you will go to bed. The presence
of the priesthood en masse might give the impression that
they have brought suit against the power of the church, and
that is inadmissible."

"They will think the same thing in any case," Father Villaverde insisted.

"I am the priest responsible for the parish, and I must go
alone, all the more so because I feel responsible to some extent for what has happened in Tajimaroa."

"You've got a case of too many scruples. You saved the
lives of Don Ulises's family and his bodyguards."

I went out into the cloister, where the police were waiting.

"Let's go," I told them, putting on my hat. "I'm at your
orders."

There were still some people in front of the palace. The
firemen who had come from Mexico City and Morelia were
putting out the remains of the fire, and the flames traced
golden arabesques on the water they profusely applied. Soldiers armed with bayonets and secret police were leading
the townspeople away—there were plenty of informers, as

was to be expected—and people voiced indignant exclamations.

In the mayor's office the state's attorney was taking statements from those detained. A man of no more than forty, tall and stout, his dull face would have lacked definite features had not the assurance he showed been accented in him, giving him an air of ridiculous competence. With a mechanical gesture he looked at the well-manicured nails of his greasy hands, and from time to time one of his secretaries offered him an American cigarette. He smoked it complacently, blowing little smoke rings that dissipated slowly in the charged atmosphere of the office.

The story of the state's attorney—which I will allow myself to summarize for Your Grace—does not differ from the story of those dozens of lawyers who have no office or clients, who begin their professional life by intriguing in the Morelia cafés with the hope of achieving a political career.

During his youth, since the government was by turns revolutionary and even socialist, he thought it was his duty to study Marxism, and he was forever speaking of the class struggle and the victory of the proletariat, which he judged imminent. Later, owing to the fatal circumstances that governments apparently lean toward the right, our young man not only burned his infamous books in the courtyard of his home, surrounded by the greatest secrecy, but also transformed himself into a supporter of order, of the principle of authority, and of police methods.

He did not—we must say it in his honor—embrace the new doctrine in a superficial manner. Now he believed (and he asserted it vigorously) that the government continued to be a revolutionary government, a democratic government that based its smallest acts on the constitution, and in order to support these assertions, he sacrificed part of his time to study the election laws with the object of justifying (keeping the appearance of legality) the appointment of official candidates, or of finding in the constitution and the legal codes those articles capable of suppressing strikes or jailing rebels that did not conflict with his revolutionary convictions.

As I entered the mayor's office, the state's attorney was questioning one of my parishioners, and he pretended not to notice my presence. The questions, as a matter of fact, recorded some facts that were insufficient to establish the man's vigorous personality—forty-five years old, married, five children. He did not smoke marijuana—"That question is offensive, señor procurador"—nor did he drink alcohol—"Well, I don't drink alcohol, just tequila or beer, now and then"— he earned six pesos per day and called himself a businessman, an honorable title with which he disguised his occupation of selling watermelons, or to be more precise, of selling watermelon slices in the plaza at Tajimaroa.

He had finished selling his melons and was already preparing to leave, when a man he did not know approached him, saying "What are you doing here? Don't you know your uncle has been killed by Don Ulises's bodyguard?"

"Ay, señor procurador, I swear to you that I simply saw red and, taking my knife, I went running to the boss's house."

"I beg you," said the state's attorney, interrupting his story, "not to refer in that way to Don Ulises Roca."

"So he was a boss, as you are an attorney, and there's God in the heavens."

"We—ell, save your comments and go on with your statement," the attorney went on, absorbed in the contemplation of his nails.

"The first thing, at his house, the priest took my knife away. Isn't it true, señor cura, that you took my knife away?"

"That is true," I replied.

"Inside, the bullets were bouncing like hail, and I was afraid."

"Ah," exclaimed the attorney, "you were afraid!"

"Not for myself, but for my children who might be orphaned."

He wiped away his perspiration with the back of his hand and went on:

"I left there, dragging myself along, and went to my uncle's house. He was very ill, almost dying, and I stayed there, not leaving his bedside, until eight o'clock at night, when I set out for the Ayuntamiento to say a rosary for the soul of Don Ulises."

Only then did the attorney appear to be aware of my presence. He left the table and, raising his hands to accentuate his pretended shock, addressed me:

"It's amazing, señor cura, the most amazing thing I've heard. First he wants to kill Don Ulises, then he says a rosary over his body. There's no doubt we're dealing with a pious man!"

"Can I go?" asked the watermelon seller.

"Certainly not, my friend, you will remain under arrest."

He paused while the soldiers led the abject businessman away and then sat down beside me.

"Forgive me for having troubled you by making you come here, but I wanted to know your opinion of these events."

"It's my opinion that the whole town rose up to kill Don Ulises."

"Actually," he corrected himself, making a gesture of displeasure, "what I am asking for is your help instead of your opinion. Could you give us a clue, any evidence that will allow us to find the perpetrator of his murder? You were with the men who were shooting at the house."

"The whole town was there."

"This town, señor cura, or these parishioners of yours, are terrible, terrible and dangerous."

"They are no better or no worse than in other parishes in the diocese, señor procurador."

"Yes, these are worse. The fact that they belong to a volcanic region makes them explosive and cruel. There are precedents for their cruelty, for their homicidal fury."

"It's not possible to condemn an entire town!"

"That's not my intention. The Michoacán prisons would not be sufficient to hold all your parishioners."

"In that case, you must pardon them all. There are also the precedents of kings and princes who bowed down before their people's justice."

"The law has nothing to do with literature. You forget, señor cura, that I am the representative of society in general and, in this particular case, of an aggrieved society. My duty consists of making sure that the principle of authority is respected, that justice is done, and with the impossibility of jailing the whole town I am going to limit myself to establishing the existence of crimes that have been sufficiently proved. On the guilty will fall the full weight of the law."

"Like that poor watermelon seller, they turn out to be the least guilty."

"Certainly. I agree you are right. It's a case of punishment that is merely a symbol and a warning, because if we did not punish them now, tomorrow they would seize the governor's palace by blood and fire."

"It's late," I told him, desirous of putting an end to the interview, "and I must go to bed."

"No one is stopping you," he hurried to say in a tone in which I noticed a bit of spite. "Later on, if we need a formal statement, I'll order you to make one in court. Meanwhile, you are free on condition that you do not leave the state."

"Good night, señor procurador."

"Good night, señor cura," he said, rising and returning to his table without offering me his hand.

53

I left the Ayuntamiento at two in the morning. I felt feverish. Chills ran down my back. My blood was pounding, beating in my temples, and I felt the seams in my skull creaking.

I needed to stay out in the garden that was caressed by shadows, to breathe the cool night air, and I leaned against a tree trunk. On the dark sky were still projected the flames that danced like will-o'-the-wisps in the burned-out framework of the sawmill. Don Ulises's house lay in ruins in the darkness, empty and repulsive.

I saw myself in my old Panama hat and my badly cut black suit, picking up my suitcase in the station at Pénjamo and going out into the sordid streets, saying: "My duty is to save the world, and if I don't save it, it will be my own fault."

Nothing remained now of that burning desire for struggle. The land of Mexico—the land crushed under the weight of poverty and injustice, our land which demands the sacrifice of heroes in order to be saved—had destroyed me, because I was half a saint, half a hero, a poor soul who had not the strength to conquer that current composed of anger, of frustrated hopes, and of bloody slime in which armed warfare, religious persecution, and agrarian reform had been dissolved. The boss's rule had signified my last opportunity, and I lost it as I had the others. Instead of leading the young men and suffering the consequences of their rebellion, I had incited it without any risk, in the protection of my cloister. Manuel, the hero, was dead, and the state's attorney, regarding his manicured nails, was selecting the victims who were to bear the blame for all of us.

There was still time to return to the Ayuntamiento and shout in his face:

"Señor procurador, order these men freed. I do not doubt that they are guilty, but there are a hundred, a thousand, ten thousand men guiltier than the thirty victims chosen by your incorruptible sense of justice. The entire town is responsible for the death of the boss and Avelino, for the fire and destruction of property, and if you are the instrument of the law, the attorney who judges an act of lawlessness, you must jail the whole town. What are you telling me? That this is not possible? That there are not enough jails for this huge crowd of criminals? That confinement of the intended victims represents a warning, a merely symbolical punishment? I accept your reasons, señor procurador. I understand very well that the impossibility of jailing fifteen thousand people, that is, the whole of my parish, forces you to choose, to discriminate, but if you consider that you must proceed symbolically, I suggest to you, based on the law and not on vain presumptions, that you imprison yourself and submit yourself to a trial. Are you laughing? Do you think I have gone crazy, or that I am joking? Ah, no, señor procurador, I am speaking seriously, perfectly seriously. The guilty ones, the only ones guilty of what has taken place in Tajimaroa, are you yourselves—those of you who create bribes and swindles in order to maintain your control over simple people and make a mockery of their voting, the ones who defraud their longing to be governed by the best men, not by the worst, as is the rule in Mexico. Are you raising your manicured hands as a sign of protest? Do you say I am insulting you? Nothing is further from my intentions, señor procurador. Not as a priest, but as a simple citizen, because of the impossibility of jailing the ones who are guilty of these crimes, I too choose you for the propitiatory victim, and I ask that your head be the one to expiate the guilt of your fellows. I have succeeded in making you angry. What do you say? That you're not angry? That your conscience as a revolutionary does not reproach you for anything? That each accusation is based on a crime that is sufficiently proved? Well, look over your records once more. You yourself obliged them to establish their identity card, those gross, blurred features like the impression left by their fingers on stamped official paper. They are almost all illiterates, men condemned to poverty from birth to death, without opportunities, without books, without lofty examples, whose destiny is to suffer illness, hunger, little official thefts, little swindles, little wrongs, little disgraces. When did you render them an account of their money? When did you worry about them? They are useful only when it is time to vote in your prefabricated elections, when it is time to pay taxes, when you extract their last centavos. Must they still tolerate a man posing as their master, thanks to his machine gun, and must they still pay for his drunken bodyguards and tax collectors and thieving policemen? Ah, señor procurador, this was too much. You must agree with me that it was too much. My parishioners are not born criminals, they are not the violent children of this volcanic region to whom you scornfully referred, but common, everyday men and women, the people, the plain people who figure so much in your speeches, in your civic festivals and in your patriotic exaltations of the country, this people of Tajimaroa, señor procurador, who once in thirty years asked for justice and, since you did not fully give it to them, took it by their own hands, destroying the chief's rule forever."

My brave sermons, my exalted defense of those who suffer wrongs and humiliations, all those dreams that expressed the best part of my nature, fell on the sterile rocks of fear and never prospered.

There was nothing to do. The first victims, among whom I distinguished the corpulent figure of the watermelon seller, came out of the palace guarded by soldiers and were lined up at the entrance, waiting for the police vans which were going to take them to jail in Morelia. I had to make a decision. At least there remained the opportunity of consoling them, of giving them my blessing, of standing beside them, since their guilt, after all, was my own guilt, and I stepped forward a few paces. At that moment the residents who were waiting in front of the palace—the majority of them relatives of the prisoners—tried to approach them, no doubt for the purpose of saying good-bye or delivering money to them, but the soldiers came between them and, shoving with their gun butts, pushed them back to the end of the plaza.

The officer in charge of the detachment took out his pistol

and gave an order. Spread out, marching rhythmically, the
soldiers lined up by twos at the rear, turning their faces
toward the plaza, and silence reigned again, a tense, unbearable silence, which was not an empty space, but the preparation for, and the beginning of, something that must inevitably come.

A sound of still-distant footsteps was coming nearer, increasing little by little, transforming itself into a disturbance,
and a minute later hundreds of townspeople poured into the
plaza. They came to the highway, suffocated, breathless, and
in a moment they had crossed the center strip and joined
the group of relatives who were still waiting expectantly.

One woman, her hair undone, half dressed, stretched out
her arms, crying hysterically:

"They're taking away our sons, our fathers, our brothers!"

A black sky had taken the place of the morning sky covered with dirty wool, and instead of the sun hidden by sti-
fling fog, the cold mercury lamps—the mayor had inaugu-
rated the new lighting along with the paving, and the people
were very proud of both improvements—shed a violet, ca-
daverous light which imparted a ghostly air to the crowd,
the soldiers, and the trees.

"Go home," said the officer in an uncertain voice. "The
soldiers have orders to shoot if you attack them."

"We don't intend to attack them, señor oficial," replied an
unknown old man. "We came to say good-bye to our relatives. We just came to say good-bye to them."

"You cannot come closer. That is an order."

"And you can't stop us from saying good-bye to our relatives."

"Get back, or abide by the consequences!" warned the
officer.

"Father!" cried the young policeman who in the morning
had shot at the boss's door and was himself among the prisoners. "Father, they're going to kill you. Go back!"

"No, I want to give you my blessing."

"Give it to me from there. Don't move!" the young man sobbed, falling to his knees.

The old man kept on walking, and the crowd hurried to fall in behind the moving spot that was his shirt, as if that blank canvas on which the silver mercury lights were shining might have been turned into a flag.

The soldiers inserted their cartridges. People instinctively began to sing the national anthem and continued to go forward. The men's deep voices supported, like columns, the delicate architrave of the feminine voices, and they formed a temple erected to liberty, a sonorous, almost corporeal mirage in the midst of the cold mercury lights, but the arrogant challenge of the anthem sounded in my ears like an invocation to death—was I not, perhaps, Monsignor, being the old choirmaster?—and I ran toward them, struck by a presentiment.

Shots rang out. The line "Encircle thy brow, oh fatherland . . ." toppled over, fluttering, like a dove stricken in mid-flight, and the recently poured concrete was covered with dead and wounded.

Panic took hold of everyone. I too ran to save myself in the trunk of a tree. My teeth were chattering. A penetrating anguish and horror rent my entrails, and sinking my nails in the trunk, I cried out, maddened:

"Why all this, my God, why, for what purpose? Speak one word, Lord, and my soul will be safe and sound!"

A profound silence surrounded me. The dead lay on the pavement without dignity, in confusion, shrunken and contracted, their faces livid, their mouths open and empty.

The sky was beginning to clear. In the tree branches the birds were stirring, and the parish bells were ringing for the first mass. Death demanded my services, and stepping forward, I began the prayer for the dead that cried out for mercy and took the place, once again, of the joyful songs of Easter.